THE BUFFALO HUNTER

PETER STRAUB

THE
BUFFALO
HUNTER

PETER
STRAUB

CEMETERY DANCE PUBLICATIONS

Baltimore
❖ 2012 ❖

FIRST EDITION
ISBN-13: 978-1-58767-236-1
Cemetery Dance Publications Edition 2012

The Buffalo Hunter
Copyright © 1990 by Peter Straub
Jacket art by © Rona Pondick, Double Bed, 1989
Jacket Design by Michael Fusco | mplusedesign.com
Typesetting and book design by Robert Morrish

Cemetery Dance Publications
132-B Industry Lane, Unit 7
Forest Hill, MD 21050
Email: info@cemeterydance.com
www.cemeterydance.com

Dedication

For Rona Pondick

I

At the peasant's words…undefined but significant ideas seemed to burst out as though they had been locked up, and all striving toward one goal, they thronged whirling through his head, blinding him with their light.

—LEO TOLSTOY, Anna Karenina

BOB BUNTING'S PARENTS SURPRISED him with a telephone call on the Sunday that was his thirty-fifth birthday. It was his first conversation with his parents in three years, though he had received a monthly letter from them during this period, along with cards on his birthdays. These usually reflected his father's abrasive comic style. Bunting had written back with the same frequency, and it seemed to him that he had achieved a perfect relationship with his parents. Separation was health; independence was health.

During his twenties, when he was sometimes between jobs and was usually short of money, he had flown from New York to spend Thanksgivings and Christmases with his parents in Michigan—Battle Creek, Michigan. Thanksgiving disappeared first, when Bunting finally got a job he liked, and in his thirtieth year Bunting had realized how he could avoid making the dreary Christmas journey into the dark and frigid Midwest. It was to this inspiration that his father referred after wishing him what sounded to Bunting like a perfunctory and insincere Happy Birthday and alluding to the rarity of their telephone conversations.

"I suppose Veronica keeps you pretty busy, huh? You guys go out a lot?"

"Oh, you know," Bunting said. "About the usual."

Veronica was entirely fictional. Bunting had not had a date with a member of the opposite sex since certain disastrous experiments in high school. Over the course of a great many letters, Veronica had evolved from a vaguely defined "friend" into a tall, black-haired, Swiss-born executive of DataCom-Corp, Bunting's employer. Still somewhat vague, she looked a little like Sigourney Weaver and a little like a woman in horn-rimmed eyeglasses he had twice seen on the M104 bus. "Well, something's keeping you pretty busy, because you never answer your phone."

"Oh, Robert," said Bunting's mother, addressing her husband's implication more than his actual words. Bunting, who also had been named Robert, was supposed to be scattering some previously unsuspected wild oats.

"Sometimes I think you just lie there and listen to the phone ring," his father said, mollifying and critical at once.

"He's *busy*," his mother breathed. "You know how they are in New York."

"Do I?" his father asked. "So you went to see *Cats*, hey, Bobby? You liked it?"

Bunting sighed. "We left at the intermission." This was what he had intended to write when the next letter came due. "I liked it okay, but Veronica thought it was terrible. Anyhow, some Swiss friends of hers were in town, and we had to go downtown to meet them."

His father asked, "Girls or boys?"

"A couple, a very good-looking young couple," Bunting said. "We went to a nice new restaurant called the Blue Goose."

"Is that a Swiss restaurant, Bobby?" his mother asked, and he glanced across the room to the mantel above the unusable fireplace of his single room, where the old glass baby bottle he had used in his childhood stood beside a thrift-shop mirror. He was used to inventing details about imaginary restaurants on paper, and improvisation made him uneasy.

"No, just an American sort of a place," he said.

"While we're on the subject of Veronica, is there any chance you could bring her back here this Christmas? We'd sure like to meet the gal."

"No—no—no, Christmas is no good, you know that. She has to get back to Switzerland to see her family, it's a really big deal for her, they all troop down to the church in the snow—"

"Well, it's a kind of a big deal for us, too," his father said.

Bunting's scalp grew sweaty. He unbuttoned his shirt collar and pulled down his tie, wondering why he had answered the telephone.

"I know, but…"

None of them spoke for a moment.

"We're just grateful you write so often," his mother finally said.

"I'll get back home one of these days, you know I will. I'm just waiting for the right time."

"Well, I suggest you make it snappy," his father said. "We're both getting older."

"But thank God, you're both healthy."

"Your mother fainted in the Red Owl parking lot last week. Passed right out and banged her head. Racked up her knee, too."

"Fainted? Why did you faint?" Bunting said. He pictured his mother swaddled in bandages.

"Oh, I don't want to talk about it," she said. "It's not really serious. I can still get around, what with my cane."

"What do you mean, 'not really serious'?"

"I get a headache when I think of all those eggs I broke," she said. "You're not to worry about me, Bobby."

"You didn't even go to a doctor, did you?"

"Oh, hell, we don't need any *doctors*," said his father. "Charge you an arm and a leg for nothing. Neither one of us has been to a doctor in twenty years."

There was a silence during which Bunting could hear his father computing the cost of the call. "Well, let's wrap this up, all right?" his father said at last.

This conversation, with its unspoken insinuations, suspicions, and judgements, left Bunting feeling jittery and exhausted. He set down the telephone, rubbed his hands over his face, and stood up to pick his way through his crowded, untidy room to the mantel of the useless fireplace. He bent to look at himself in the mirror. His thinning hair stood up in little tufts where he had tortured it while talking to his parents. He pulled a comb from his jacket pocket and flattened the tufts over his scalp. His pink, inquisitive face looked reassuringly back at him from above the collar of his crisp white shirt. In honor of his birthday, he had put on a new tie and one of his best suits, a grey nail-head worsted that instantly made its wearer look like the CEO of a Fortune 500 company. He posed for a moment before the mirror, bending his knees to consult the image of his torso, neck, and boyish, balding head. Then he straightened up and looked at his watch. It was four-thirty, not too early for a birthday drink.

Bunting took his old baby bottle from the mantel and stepped over a pile of magazines to enter his tiny kitchen area and opened the freezer compartment of his refrigerator. He set the baby bottle down on the meager counter beside the sink and removed a quart bottle of Popov vodka from the freezer, which he placed beside the baby bottle. Bunting unscrewed the nipple from the bottle, inspected the pink, chewed-looking nipple and the interior of the bottle for dust and foreign substances, blew into each, and then set down bottle and nipple. He removed the cap from the vodka and tilted it over the baby bottle.

A stream of liquid like silvery treacle poured from one container into the other. Bunting half-filled the baby bottle with frigid vodka, and then, because it was his birthday, added another celebratory gurgle that made it nearly three-quarters full. He capped the vodka bottle and put it back in the otherwise empty freezer. From the refrigerator he removed a plastic bottle of Schweppes tonic water, opened it, and added tonic until the baby bottle was full. He screwed the nipple back onto the neck of the bottle and gave it two hard shakes. A little of the mixture squirted through the opening of the nipple, which Bunting had enlarged with the tip of a silver pocket-knife. The glass bottle grew cold in his hand.

Bunting skirted the wing chair that marked the boundary of his kitchen, stepped back over the mound of old newspapers, dropped the bottle on his hastily made bed, and shrugged off his suit jacket. He hung the jacket over the back of a wooden chair and sat down on the bed. There was a Luke Short novel on the rush seat of the wooden chair, and he picked it up and swung his legs onto the bed. When he leaned back into the pillows, the bottle tilted and expressed a transparent drop of vodka and tonic onto the rumpled blue coverlet. Bunting snatched up the bottle, awkwardly opened the book, and grunted with satisfaction as the words lifted, full of consolation and excitement, from the page. He brought the bottle to his mouth and began to suck cold vodka through the hole in the spongy pink nipple.

On one of his Christmas visits home, Bunting had unearthed the bottle while rummaging through boxes in the attic of his parents' house. He had not even seen it at first—a long glass shape at the bottom of a paper bag containing an empty wartime ration book, two small, worn pairs of moccasins, and a stuffed monkey, partially dismembered. He had gone upstairs to escape his father's questions and his mother's looks of worry—

Bunting at the time being employed in the mail room of a magazine devoted to masturbatory fantasies—and had become absorbed in the record of his family's past life which the attic contained. Here were piles of old winter coats, boxed photograph albums containing tiny pictures of strangers and empty streets and long-dead dogs, stacks of yellowed newspapers with giant wartime headlines (ROMMEL SMASHED! and VICTORY IN EUROPE!), paperback novels in rows against a slanting wall, bags of things swept from the backs of closets.

The monkey came firmly into this category, as did the shoes, though Bunting was not certain about the ration book. Wedged beneath the moccasins, the tubular glass bottle glinted up from the bottom of the bag. Bunting discarded the monkey, a barely remembered toy, and fished out the thick, surprisingly weighty baby bottle. An ivory-colored ring of plastic with a wide opening for a rubber nipple had been screwed down over the bottle's top. Bunting examined the bottle, realising that once, in true helplessness, he had clutched this object to his infant chest. Once his own tiny fingers had spread over the thick glass while he had nursed. This proxy, this imitation and simulated breast had kept him alive: it was a period piece, it was something like an object of everyday folk art, and it had survived when his childhood—visible now only as a small series of static moments that seemed plucked from a vast darkness—had not. Above all, perhaps, it made him smile. He held on to it as he walked around the little attic—he did not want to let go of it—and when he came back downstairs, hid it in his suitcase. And then forgot it was there.

When he got home, the baby bottle's presence in his suitcase, wrapped in a coil of dirty shirts, startled him: it was as if the glass tube had followed him from Battle Creek to Manhattan by itself. Then he remembered wrapping it in the shirts on the night before his departure, a night when his father got drunk during dinner and said three times in succession, each time louder than the last, "I don't think you're ever going to amount to anything in this world, Bobby," and his mother started crying, and his father got disgusted with them both and stomped outside to lurch around in the snow. His mother had gone upstairs to the bedroom, and Bunting had switched on the television and sat without feeling before depictions of other people's Christmases. Eventually his father had come back inside and joined him in front of the television without speaking to him or even looking at him. At the airport the next morning, his father had scratched his face in a whiskery embrace and said that it had been good to see him again, and his mother looked brave and stricken. They were two old people, and working-class Michigan seemed unbearably ugly, with an ugliness he remembered.

He put the bottle away in a cupboard on a high shelf and forgot about it again.

Over the following years, Bunting saw the bottle only on the few occasions he had to reach for something on its shelf. He either ate most of his meals in inexpensive neighbourhood restaurants or ordered them from Empire Szechuan, so he had little use for the pots and pans that stood there. During these years he found the job in the mail room of DataComCorp, invented Veronica for his parents' pleasure and his own, reduced and then finally terminated his visits to Michigan, moved into his early thirties, and settled into what he imagined were the habits of his adult life.

He saved his money, having little to spend it on apart from his rent. Every autumn and every spring, he went to a good men's clothing store and bought two suits, several new shirts, and three or four new neckties: these excursions were great adventures, and he prepared for them carefully, examining advertisements and comparing the merits of the goods displayed at Barneys, Paul Stuart, Polo, Armani, and two or three other shops he considered to be in their class. He read the same Westerns and mystery novels his father had once read. He ate his two meals a day in the fashion described. His hair was cut once every two weeks by a Japanese barber around the corner who remarked on the smoothness of his collar as he tucked the protective sheet next to his neck. He washed his dishes only when they were all used up, and once a month or so he swept the floor and put things into piles. He set out roach killer and mousetraps and closed his eyes when he disposed of corpses. No one but himself ever entered his apartment, but at work he sometimes talked with Frank Herko, the man at the next word processor. Frank envied Bunting's wardrobe, and swapped tales of his own sex life, conducted in bars and discos, for Bunting's more sedate accounts of evenings with Veronica.

Bunting liked to read lying down, and liked to drink while he read. His little apartment was cold in the winter, and the only place to lie down in it was the bed, so for four months of every year, Bunting spent much of every weekend and most of his evenings wrapped up fully clothed in his blankets, a glass of cold vodka (without tonic, for this was after Labor Day) in one hand, a paperback book in the other. The only difficulty with this system, otherwise perfectly adapted to Bunting's desires and needs, had been the occasional spillage. There had been technical problems concerning the uprightness of the glass during the turning of the pages. One solution was to prop the glass against the side of his body as he turned the page, but this method met with frequent failure, as did the technique of balancing the glass on his chest. Had he cleared all the books, wads of Kleenex used and unused, pill bottles, cotton balls, ear cleaners, jar of Vaseline, and the hand mirror from the chair beside his bed, he could have placed the glass on the seat between sips; but he did not want to have to reach for his drink. Bunting wanted his satisfactions prompt and ready to hand.

Depending on the time of the day, the drink Bunting might choose to go with *New Gun in Town* or *Saddles and Sagebrush* could be herbal tea, orange juice, warm milk, Tab or Pepsi-Cola, mineral water: should he not be enabled to take in such pleasurable and harmless liquids without removing his eye from the page? Every other area of life was filled with difficulty and compromise; this—bed and a book—should be pristine.

The solution came to him one November after a mysterious and terrifying experience that occurred as he was writing his monthly letter home.

Dear Mom and Dad,

Everything is still going so well I sometimes think I must be dreaming. Veronica says she has never seen any employee anywhere come so far so fast. We went dancing at the Rainbow Room last night following dinner at Quaglino's, a new restaurant all the critics are raving about. As I walked her back to Park Avenue through the well-dressed crowds on Fifth Avenue, she told me that she felt she would once again really need me by her side in Switzerland this Christmas, it's hard for her to defend herself against her brother's charges that she has sold out her native country, and the local aristocracy is all against her too...

The mention of Christmas caused him to see, as if printed on a postcard, the image of the dingy white house in Battle Creek, with his parents standing before the front steps, his father scowling beneath the bill of a plaid cap and his mother blinking with apprehension. They faced forward, like the couple in *American Gothic.* He stopped writing and his mind spun past them up the steps, through the door, up the stairs into a terrifying void. For a moment he thought he was going to faint, or that he *had* fainted. Distant white lights wheeled above him, and he was falling through space. Some massive knowledge moved within him, thrusting powerfully upward from the darkness where it had been jailed, and he understood that his life depended on keeping this knowledge locked inside him, in a golden casket within a silver casket within a leaden casket. It was a wild beast with claws and teeth, a tiger, and this tiger had threatened to surge into his conscious mind and destroy him. Bunting was panting from both the force and the threat of the tiger locked within him, and he was looking at the white paper where his pen had made a little scratchy scrawl after the word *too,* aware that he had not fainted—but it was, just then and only for a second, as if his body had been hurled through some dark barrier.

Drained, he lay back against the headboard and tried to remember what had just happened. It was already blurred by distance. He had seen his parents and flown...? He remembered the expression on his mother's face, the blinking, almost simian eyes and the deep parallel lines in her forehead, and felt his heart beating with the relief that he had escaped whatever it was that had surged up from within him. So thoroughly had he escaped it that he now wondered about the reality of his experience. A thick shield had slammed back into place, where it emphatically belonged.

And then came Bunting's revelation.

He thought of the old baby bottle on its shelf and saw how he could use it. He set aside the letter and went across his room to take down the bottle from its high shelf. It came away from the shelf with a faint kissing sound.

The bottle was covered with fluffy grey dust, and a sticky brown substance from the shelf circled its base. Bunting squeezed dishwashing liquid into the bottle and held it under a stream of hot water. He scrubbed the bottom clean, unscrewed the plastic cap, and washed the grooves on the cap and the neck of the bottle. As he dried the warm bottle with his clean dish towel, he saw his mother bent over the sink in her dark little kitchen, her arms sunk into soapy water and steam rising past her head.

Bunting thrust this image away and regarded the bottle. It seemed surprisingly beautiful for so functional an object. The bottle was a perfect cylinder of clear glass, which sparkled as it dried. Oddly, its smooth, caressing weight felt as comfortable in his adult hand as it must have in his childish one. The plastic cap twirled gracefully down over the moulded 'O' of the bottle's mouth. One tiny air bubble had been caught ascending from the thick rim at the bottom. The manufacturer's name, Prentiss, was spelled out in thick transparent letters circling the bottle's shoulders.

He placed it on the cleanest section of the counter and squatted to admire his work. The bottle was an obelisk made of a miraculous transparent skin. The wall behind it turned to a swarmy, elastic blur. For a moment Bunting wished that his two windows, which looked out onto a row of decrepit brownstones on the west side of Manhattan, were of the same thick, distorting glass.

He went out onto Eighth Avenue to search for nipples, and found them in a drugstore, hanging slightly above eye level, wrapped in packages of three like condoms, and surrounded by a display of bottles. He snatched the first pack of nipples off the hook and carried it to the register. He practiced what he would say if the sullen Puerto Rican girl asked him why he was buying baby bottle nipples—*Darn kid goes through these things in a hurry*—but she charged him ninety-six cents, pushed the package into a bag, took his dollar, and gave him change without a comment or even a curious glance.

He carried the bag back to his building rejoicing, as if he had narrowly escaped some great danger. The ice had not broken beneath his feet: he was in command of his life.

At home, he drew the package of nipples from the bag and noticed first that they were stacked vertically, like the levels of a pagoda, secondly that they were Evenflo nipples, "designed especially for juice." That was all right, he was going to use them to get juiced.

Dear Parent, read the back of the package, *All babies are unique.* Bunting cheered the wise patriarchs of the Evenflo Products Company. The Evenflo system let you adjust the flow rate to ensure that Baby always got a smooth, even flow. *Baby swallows less air, too.* Sure-Seal nipples had twin air valves. They were called the Pacers, as if they were members of a swift, confident family.

Bunting was warned not to put the nipples into microwave ovens, and cautioned that every nipple wore out. There was an 800 number to call, if you had questions.

He took his quart of Popov from the freezer and carefully decanted vodka into the sparkling bottle. The clear liquid sprang to the top and formed a trembling meniscus above the glass mouth. Bunting used his pocket-knife to cut the nipples from the pack, taking care to preserve the instructions for their use, and removed the topmost level of the pagoda. The nipple felt surprisingly firm and resilient between his fingers. Impatiently, he fitted the nipple into the cap ring and screwed the ring down onto the bottle. Then he tilted it to his mouth and sucked.

The nipple met his teeth and tongue, which instantly accepted it, for what suits a mouth better than a nice new nipple? But a frustratingly thin stream of vodka came through the crosscut opening. Bunting sucked harder, working the nipple between his teeth like gum, but the vodka continued to stream through the opening at the same even, deliberate rate.

Now Bunting took his little silver knife, actually Frank Herko's, from his pocket. Bunting had seen it lying on Herko's desk for several days before borrowing it. He intended to give it back someday, but no one could dispute that the elegant knife suited someone like Bunting far more than Frank Herko— in fact, Herko had probably found it on a sidewalk, or beneath a table in a restaurant (for Frank Herko really did go to restaurants, the names of which Bunting appropriated for his tales of Veronica), and therefore it was as much Bunting's as his. Very cautiously, Bunting inserted the delicate blade into one of the smooth crosscut incisions. He lengthened the cut in the rubber by perhaps an eighth of an inch, then did the same to the other half of the crosscut. He replaced the nipple in the cap ring, tightened the ring onto the bottle, and tested his improvement.

A mouthful of vodka slipped through the enlarged opening and chilled his teeth.

Bunting had taken his wonderful new invention directly to bed, shedding his tie and his jacket as he went. He picked up his Luke Short novel and sucked vodka through the nipple. When he turned the page, he clamped the nipple between his teeth and let the bottle dangle, jutting downward past his lower lip like a monstrous cigar. A feeling of discontinuity, unfinished business, troubled him. He was riding down onto a grassy plateau atop a dun horse named Shorty. He gazed out across a herd of grazing buffalo. The bottle dangled again as the bottom half of the letter to his parents slipped down his legs into the herd of buffalo. "Oh," he said. "Oh, yes."

The baby bottle, inspired by the event which had befallen him as he wrote the letter, had *replaced* it. All Bunting wanted to do was luxuriate in his bed, rolling atop old Shorty, clutching his trusty bottle in pursuit of buffalo hides, but more than a sense of duty compelled him to fold down the corner of the page and close the book on Shorty and the browsing herd. Bunting's heart had lightened. He picked up the pad on which he had been writing to faraway Battle Creek, found his pen in the folds of the blanket, and resumed writing.

So I'll have to go with her again, he wrote, then dropped down the page to begin a paragraph dictated from the center of his new satisfaction.

Have I ever really told you about Veronica, Mom and Dad? I mean, really told you about her? Do you know how beautiful she is, and how intelligent, and how successful? I bet not a day goes by that some photographer doesn't ask her to pose for him, or an editor doesn't stop her on the street to say that she has to be on the cover of his magazine. She has dark hair and high, wide cheekbones, and sometimes I think she looks like a great cat getting ready to spring. She has a MBA, and she reads a novel in one day. She does all the crossword puzzles in ink. And fashion sense! It's no wonder she looks like a model! You look at those top models in the newspaper ads, the ones with long dark hair and full lips, and you'll see her, you'll see how graceful Veronica is. The way she bends, the way she moves, the way she holds her glasses in one hand, and how cute she looks when she looks out through them, just like a beautiful kitten. And she loves this country, Dad, you should hear her talk about the benefits America gives its people— honestly, there's never been a girl like this before, and I thank my stars I found her and won her love.

With this letter Bunting had come into his own. Despite all the lies he had told about her, lies that had become woven into his life so deeply that a beautiful shadow had seemed to accompany him on the bus back and forth to work, Veronica had never been so present to him, so visible. She had come out of the shadows.

He continued:

In fact, my relationship with Veronica is getting better and better. She gives me what I need, that comfort and stability you need when you come home from the business world, close your door behind you, and want to be free from the troubles and pressures of the day. Did I tell you about the way she'll pout at me in the middle of some big meeting with a DataComCorp client, just a little tiny movement that no one but me would possibly notice? It gives me the shivers, Mom and Dad. And she has shown me so much of the life and excitement of this town, the ins and outs of having fun in the Big Apple—I really think this is going to last, and one fine day I'll probably pop the question! She'd say yes in a minute, I know, because she really does love me as much as I love her—

II

BUNTING WOKE UP WITH A HANGOVER
on the Monday after his birthday and immediately
decided that it would not be necessary to go to work.

His room offered evidence of a disorderly night.
The Popov bottle, nearly empty, stood on the counter beside the refrigerator, and one of his lamps had
been on all night, shedding a yellow circle of light
upon a mass of folds and wrinkles that resolved into
his grey worsted suit from Paul Stuart. Evidently
he had tossed aside the jacket, undone his belt, and
stepped out of his trousers as he moved toward the
bed. His shoes lay widely separated, as if he had torn
them off his feet and tossed them away. Closer to the
bed were his tie, yesterday's white shirt, and his underwear, all of which formed points on a line leading
toward his poisoned body. Beside him lay the empty
Prentiss baby bottle and a paperback copy of *The
Buffalo Hunter*, splayed open on the sheet. Evidently
he had tried to read after finally getting out of his
clothes and making it to bed: his body had followed
its habits although his mind had stopped working.

He moved his legs off the bed, and sudden nausea made him fear that he was going to vomit before
he could get to the toilet. The clarity he had experienced on first waking vanished into headache and
other physical miseries. Some other, more decayed
body had replaced the one he knew. The nausea
ebbed away, and Bunting pushed himself off the

bed. He looked down at long white skinny legs. These were certainly not his. The legs took him to the bathroom, where he sat on the toilet. He heard himself moaning. Eventually he was able to get into the shower, where the hot water sizzled down on the stranger's body. The stranger's wrinkled hands pushed soap across his white skin and rubbed shampoo into his lifeless hair.

Slowly, he dressed himself in a dark suit, a clean white shirt, and a navy blue necktie with white stripes, the clothes he would have worn to a funeral. His head seemed to float farther from the ground than he remembered, and his arms and legs were spindly and breakable. Bunting experienced a phantasmal happiness, a ghastly good cheer released by the disappearance of so much of his everyday self.

The mirror showed him a white, aged Bunting with sparkling eyes. He was still a little drunk, he realized, but did not remember why he'd had so much of the vodka—he wondered if there had been a reason and decided that he had simply celebrated his birthday too vigorously. "Thirty-five," he said to the white spectre in the mirror. "Thirty-five and one day." Bunting was not accustomed to giving much attention to any birthdays or anniversaries, even his own, and only the call from Battle Creek had reminded him that anyone else knew that the day was anything but ordinary. He had not even given himself a present.

That was how he would spend this peculiar morning. He would buy himself a thirty-fifth birthday present. Then, if he felt more like himself, he would go in to work.

Bunting located his sunglasses on his dining table, pushed them into his breast pocket, and let himself out of his room. The corridor looked even shabbier than usual. Sections of wallpaper curled down from the seams and corners, and whole sections of the wall had been spray-painted with puffy, cartoonish nonsense words. BANGO SKANK. JEEPY. Bunting's feeling of breakability increased. He worked his way through the murk of the hallway to the elevator and pushed the button several times. A few minutes later, he stepped out of the elevator and permitted himself to breathe. After the elevator, the lobby smelled like a freshly mown hayfield. Two ripped couches of imitation leather faced each other across a dirty stone floor. A boxy wooden desk stood empty against a grey wall miraculously kept clean of graffiti. A six-foot fern was turning a crisp, pale brown in a pot beside the desk.

Bunting pushed his way through the smudgy glass doors, then the heavy wooden doors past the row of buzzers, and came out into bright sunlight that instantly bounced into his eyes from the tops of a dozen cars, from clean shop windows, from the steel wristbands of watches and glittering earrings, from a hundred bright things large and small. Bunting yanked his sunglasses from his pocket and put them on.

When he passed the drugstore, he remembered that he needed a new pack of nipples, and turned in. Inside, a slanted mirror gave him a foreshortened version of himself, all bulging forehead and sinister glasses. He looked like an alien being in disguise. Bunting walked through the glaring aisles to the back of the store and the displays of goods for infants.

Here were the wonderful siblings of the Pacer family, but as he reached for them, he saw what he had missed the first time. The drugstore carried not only the orange nipples with the special cross-cut opening, but in rows on both sides of the juice nipples, flesh-colored nipples for drinking formula, white nipples for drinking milk, and blue nipples for drinking water.

He took down packets of each kind of nipple, and then realized that perfect birthday presents were hanging all over the wall before him. On his first visit, he had not even noticed all the baby bottles displayed alongside the nipples; he had not been interested in baby bottles then, apart from his own. He had not imagined that he would ever be interested in other baby bottles. And in other ways also he had been mistaken. He had assumed that baby bottles remained the same over time, like white dress shirts and black business shoes and hardcover books, that the form had been perfected sometime early in the twentieth century and seventy or eighty years later was simply reproduced in larger numbers. This had been an error. Baby bottles were objects like automobiles and breakfast cereals, capable of astonishing variation.

Smiling with this astonished pleasure, Bunting walked up and down past the display, carrying his packets of white, orange, blue, and flesh-colored nipples. The first transformation in bottles had been in shape, the second in material, the third in color. There had also been an unexplained change of manufacturers. None of these bottles before him were Prentiss baby bottles. Every single one was made either by Evenflo or Playtex. What had happened to Prentiss? The manufacturers of his long-lasting, extremely serviceable bottle had gone out of business—skunked, flushed, busted.

Bunting felt a searing flash of shame for his parents: they had backed a loser.

Most baby bottles were not even round anymore. They were six-sided, except for those (Easy Hold) that looked like elongated doughnuts, with a long narrow oval in the middle through which a baby's fingers could presumably slide. And the round ones, the Playtex bottles, were nothing more than shells around collapsible plastic bags. These hybrid objects, redolent of menopausal old age, made Bunting shudder. Of the six-sided bottles—nursers, as they were now called—some were yellow, others orange, and some had a row of little smiling faces marching up the ounce markings on the side. Some of these new types of bottles were glass, but most were made of a thin transparent plastic.

Bunting instantly understood that, except for the ones that contained the collapsing breast, he had to have all of these bottles. Even his headache seemed to loosen its grip. He had found the perfect birthday present for himself. Now that he had seen them, it was not possible not to buy one each of most of these varieties of "nursers." Another brilliant notion penetrated him, as if sent by arrow from a heavenly realm.

He saw lined up on the shelf beside his stove a bottle for coffee and one for tea, a bottle for cold vodka, another for nice warm milk, bottles for soft drinks and different kinds of beer and one for mineral water, a library of bottles. There could be morning bottles and evening bottles and late-night bottles. He'd need a lot more nipples, he realized, and began taking things down from their hooks.

Back in his apartment, Bunting washed his birthday presents and set them out on his counter. The row did not look as imposing as he had envisioned it would—there were only seven bottles in all, his old Prentiss and six new ones. Seven seemed too few. He remembered all the bottles left on the wall. He should have bought more of them. A double row of bottles—"nursers"—would be twice as impressive. It was his birthday, wasn't it?

Still, he had a collection—a small collection. He ran his fingers over the row of bottles and selected one made of clear plastic, to sample the difference between it and the old round glass Prentiss. Because he felt a bit dehydrated, he filled it with tap water and pushed a blue Water Nipple through the cap ring. The new nipple was deliciously slippery on his tongue. Bunting yawned, and half-consciously took the new blue-tipped bottle to his bed. He promised himself he would lie down for just a few minutes, and collapsed onto the unmade bed. He opened his book, began to suck water through the new nipple, and fell asleep so immediately and thoroughly he might have been struck in the back of the head with a mallet.

When Bunting awoke two hours later, he could not remember exactly where, or even exactly who, he was. Nothing around him looked familiar. The light—more precisely, the relative quality of the darkness—was all wrong. He did not understand why he was wearing a suit, a shirt, a tie, and shoes, and he felt some deep, mysterious sense of shame. He had betrayed himself, he had been *found out*, and now he was in disgrace. His mouth tasted terrible. Gradually, his room took shape around him, but it was the wrong time for this room. Why wasn't he at work? His heart began to beat faster. Bunting sat up, groaning, and saw the rank of sparkling new baby bottles, each with its new nipple, beside his sink. The sense of shame and disgrace retreated. He remembered that he had taken the morning off, and for a moment thought that he really should write a letter to his parents as soon as his head cleared.

But he had just talked to his parents. He had escaped another Christmas, though this was balanced by some alarming news his father had given to him. The exact nature of this news would not yield itself: it felt like a large, tender bruise, and his mind recoiled from the memory of injury.

He looked at his watch, and was surprised that it was only eleven-thirty.

Bunting got out of bed, thinking that he might as well go to work. In the bathroom, he splashed water on his face and brushed his teeth, taking care not to get water or toothpaste on his jacket or tie. While he gargled mouthwash, he remembered: his mother had fallen down in some supermarket parking lot. Had his father insinuated that he ought to come back to Battle Creek? No, there had been no such insinuation. He was sure of that. And what could he do to help his mother, even if he went back? She was all right—what she had really minded was breaking a lot of eggs.

III

AN ODDLY ENERGETIC EXHILARATION, as if he had narrowly escaped some great danger, came to Bunting when he walked back out into the sunlight, and when his bus did not arrive immediately, he found himself walking to DataComCorp's offices. His body felt in some way still not his, but capable of moving at a good rate down the sidewalks toward Columbus Circle and then midtown. The mid-autumn air felt fresh and cool, and the memory of the six new baby bottles back in his apartment was a bubbling inner spring, surfacing in his thoughts, then disappearing underground before coming to the surface again.

Did ever a young mother go into a drugstore in search of a baby bottle for her new infant, and not find one?

Bunting arrived at the door of the Data Entry room just at the time that one of his fellow workers was leaving with orders for sandwiches and drinks. Few of Bunting's fellow workers chose to spend their salaries on restaurant lunches, and nearly all of them ate delicatessen sandwiches in a group by the coffee machine or alone at their desks. Bunting generally ate in his cubicle or in Frank Herko's, for Frank disdained most of their fellow clerks, as did Bunting. Though some of the other clerks had attended trade or technical schools, only Bunting and Frank Herko had been to college. Bunting had two

34

years at Lansing College, Herko, two at Yale. Frank Herko looked nothing like Bunting's idea of a Yale student. He was stocky and barrel-chested, with a black beard and long, curly black hair. He generally dressed in baggy trousers and shabby sweaters, some with actual holes in the wool. Neither did Herko behave like his office friend's idea of a Yalie, being aggressive, loud, and frank to the point of crudity. Bunting had been disturbed and annoyed by Herko during his first months in Data Entry, an attitude undermined and finally changed by the other man's persistent, oddly delicate deference, friendliness, and curiosity. Herko had seemed to decide that the older man was a sort of treasure, a real *rara avis*, deserving of special treatment.

Bunting asked the messenger to bring him a Swiss cheese and Black Forest ham sandwich on whole wheat, mustard and mayonnaise, lettuce and tomato. "Oh, and coffee," he said. "Black coffee."

Herko was winding his way toward the door, beaming at him. "Uh huh, black coffee," he said. "You *look* like black coffee today. Nice of you to make it in, Bunting, my man. I take it you had an unusually late night."

"You could say that."

"Oh yes, oh yes. And we show up for work right after getting out of bed, don't we? With our beautiful suit all covered in wrinkles from the night before."

"Well," Bunting said, looking down. Long pronounced wrinkles ran down the length of the suit jacket, intersecting longitudinal wrinkles that matched other wrinkles in his tie. He had been too disoriented to notice them when he had awakened from his nap. "I did just get out of bed." He began trying to smooth out the wrinkles in his jacket.

Frank took a step nearer and sniffed the air. "A stench of alcohol is still oozing from the old pores. Had a little party, didn't we?" He bent toward Bunting and peered into his face. "My God. You really look like shit, you know that? Why'd you come to work anyhow, you dumb fuck? You couldn't take a day off?"

"I wanted to come to work," Bunting said. "I took the morning off, didn't I?"

"Rolling around in bed with the beautiful Veronica," Herko said. "Hurry up and get into your cubicle before one of the old cunts gets a whiff of you and keels over."

He propelled Bunting toward his row and cubicle. Bunting pushed open his door and fell into the chair facing his terminal. A stack of paper several inches high had been placed beside his keyboard.

Herko pulled a tube of Binaca from his trousers pocket. "For God's sake, give yourself a shot of this, will you?"

"I brushed my teeth," Bunting protested. "Twice."

"Use it anyhow. Keep it. You're going to need it."

Bunting dutifully squirted cinnamon-flavoured vapour onto his tongue and put the tube in his jacket pocket.

"Bunting cuts loose," Herko said. "Bunting gets down and dirty. Bunting the party animal." He was grinning. "Did Veronica do a number on you, or did you do a number on her, man?"

Bunting rubbed his eyes.

"Hey, man, you can't just show up in last night's clothes, still wasted from the night before, on top of everything else three hours late!—and not expect me to be curious." He leaned forward and stretched out his arms, enlarging the baggy blue sweater. "Talk to me! What the hell happened? Did you and Veronica have an anniversary or a fight?"

"Neither one," said Bunting.

Herko put his hands on his hips and shook his head, silently pleading for more of the story.

"Well, I was somewhere else," Bunting said.

"Obviously. You sure as hell didn't go *home* last night."

"And I was with someone else," Bunting said.

Herko crowed and balled his fist and pumped his arm, elbow bent. "Attaboy. Attaway. Bunting's on a roll."

Again Bunting saw his parents posed before their peeling house like the couple in *American Gothic*, his father on the verge of uttering some banal heartlessness and his mother virtually twitching with anxiety. They were small, Bunting realized, the size of dolls.

"I've been seeing a couple of new people. Now and then. Off and on."

"A couple of new people?" Herko said.

"Two or three. Three, actually."

"What does Veronica have to say about that? Does she even know?"

"Veronica and I are cooling off a little bit. We're creating some space between us. She's probably seeing other people too, but she says she isn't." These inventions came easily to Bunting, and he propped his chin in the palm of his hand and looked into Frank Herko's luminous eyes. "I guess I was getting a little bored or something. I wanted some variety. You don't want the same thing all the time, do you?"

"You don't want to be stultified," Herko said quickly. "You get stultified, going with the same person all the time."

"It was always hard for Veronica to relax. People like that don't ever really slow down and take things easy. They're always thinking about getting ahead, about how to make more money, get a little more status."

"I didn't know Veronica was like that," Herko said. He had been given a very different picture of Bunting's girlfriend.

"Believe me, it even took me a long time to see it. You don't want to admit a kind of thing like that." He shrugged. "But once she starts looking around, she'll find somebody more suitable. I mean, we still love each other, but..."

"It wasn't working out, that's obvious," Herko supplied. "She wasn't right for you, she didn't have the same values, it could never turn out happily. You're doing the right thing. Besides, you're going out and having fun, aren't you? What more do you want?"

"I want my headache to go away," Bunting said. The sensation of a slight, suspended drunkenness had passed, and with it the feeling of inhabiting an unfamiliar body.

"Oh, for God's sake, why didn't you say so?" asked Herko, and disappeared into his own cubicle. Bunting could see the top of his head floating back and forth like a wig over the top of the partition. Desk drawers moved in and out. In a moment Herko was back with two aspirin, which he set atop Bunting's desk before going out to the water cooler. Bunting sat motionless as royalty. Herko returned with a conical paper cup brimming with water just as the woman came in with a cardboard box filled with the department's orders from the deli.

"Hand over our wonderful four-star lunches and leave us alone," Herko said.

They unwrapped their sandwiches and began to eat, Herko casting eager and importunate looks toward the older man. Bunting ate with fussy deliberation, and Herko chomped. There was a long silence.

"This sandwich tastes good," Bunting said at last.

"Yeah, yeah," Herko said. "Right now, *Alpo* would taste good to you. What about the girl? Tell me about the girl."

"Oh, Carol?"

"What's this 'Oh, Carol?' shit, Bunting? You think I know the girl, or something? Tell me about her—where did you meet her, how old is she, what does she do for a living, does she have good legs and big tits, you know—*tell* me!"

Bunting chewed on slowly, deliberately, regarding Herko. The younger man looked like a large, shaggy puppy. "I met her in an art gallery."

"You devil."

"I was just walking past the place, and when I looked in the window I saw her sitting behind the desk. The next day when I walked past, she was there again, so I went in and walked around, pretending to look at the pictures. I started talking with her, and then I started coming back to the gallery, and after a while I asked her out."

"Those girls in art galleries are incredible," Herko said. "That's why they're working in art galleries. You can't have a dog selling beautiful pictures, right?" He shook his head. His sandwich oozed a whitish liquid onto the thick white paper, and a trace of the liquid clung to the side of his mouth. "You know what you are, Bunting? You're a secret weapon." A bit more white liquid squirted from the corner of his mouth. "You're a goddamned *missile silo*."

"Carol is more like my kind of person, that's all," Bunting said. Secretly, this description thrilled him. "She's more like an artistic kind of person, not so into her career and everything. She's willing to focus more on me."

"Which means she's a hundred percent better in bed, am I right?"

"Well," Bunting said, thinking vaguely that Veronica had after all been very good in bed.

"It's obvious, it goes without saying," Herko said. "You don't even have to tell me."

Bunting shrugged.

"What's her last name?"

"Even," Bunting said. "Carol Even. It's an English name."

"At least English is her first language. She's a product of your own culture, of course she's more your type than some Swiss money machine. Tell me about the other two."

"Oh, you know," Bunting said. He sipped from the Styrofoam container of coffee. "It's the usual kind of thing."

"Do they all work in art galleries? Do you boff 'em all at once, or do you just take them one by one? Where do you go? Do you make the club scene? Concerts? Or do you just invite them back to your place for a nice soulful *talk?*" He was chewing frantically as he talked, waving his free hand. A pink paste filled his mouth, a pulp of compressed roast beef, mayonnaise, and whole-grain bread. "You're a madman, Bunting, you're a stone wacko. I always knew it—I knew you were gonzo from the moment you first walked into this place. You can fool all these old ladies with your fancy clothes, but I can see your fangs, my friend, and they are long, long fangs." Herko swallowed the mess in his mouth and twinkled at Bunting.

"You could see that, huh?"

"First thing. Long fangs, my friend. Now tell me about these other women." He suppressed a burp. "Go on, we only got a couple of minutes."

Lunch ended twenty minutes later, and the day slid forward. Though Bunting felt tired, his odd exhilaration had returned—an exhilaration that seemed like a freedom from some heavy, painful responsibility—and as his fingers moved across the keyboard of his computer, he thought about the women he had described to Frank Herko. Images of the wonderful new baby bottles back in his room flowed in and out of his fantasies.

He found he was making a surprising number of typing mistakes.

Late in the afternoon, Herko's head appeared over the top of the partition separating their two cubicles.

"How's it going?"

"Slowly," Bunting said.

"Forget about it, you're still convalescing. Listen, I had a great idea. You're not really going out with Veronica anymore, right?"

"I didn't say that," Bunting said.

"You know what I mean. You're basically a free man, aren't you? My friend Lindy has this girlfriend, Marty, who wants to go out with someone new. Marty's a great kid. You'd like her. That's a promise, man.

If I could, I'd take her out myself, but Lindy would kill me if I did. No kidding—I wouldn't put you on about this, I think you'd like her a lot and you could have a good time with her, and if everything works out, which I don't see why it should not, all four of us could go out somewhere together."

"Marty?" Bunting asked. "You want me to go out with someone named Marty?"

Frank snickered. "Hey, she's really cute, don't act that way with me. This is actually Lindy's idea, I guess I talked about you with her, and she thought you sounded okay, you know, so when her friend Marty started saying this and that, she was breaking up with a guy, she asked me about you. And I said no way, this guy is all wrapped up. But since you're going wild, you really ought to check Marty out. I'm not kidding."

He was not. His head looked even bigger than usual, his beard seemed to jump out of his skin, his hair foamed from his scalp, his eyes bulged. Bunting had a brief, unsettling image of what it would be like to be a girl, fending off all this insistent male energy.

"I'll think about it," he said.

"Great. Do I have your phone number? I do, don't I?"

Bunting could not remember having given Herko his telephone number—he very rarely gave it out—but he recited it to the eager head looking down at him, and the head disappeared below the partition as Herko went to his desk to write down the number. A moment later, the head reappeared. "You're not going to be sorry about this. I promise!" Herko disappeared behind the partition.

Bunting's entire body went cold. "Now, wait just a second. What are you going to do?" He could feel his heart racing.

"What do you think I'm going to do?" Herko called over the partition.

"You can't give anybody my number!" Bunting heard his own voice come up in a squeaky wail, and realized that everybody else in the Data Entry room had also heard him.

Herko's upper body appeared leaning around the door to Bunting's cubicle. He was frowning. "Hey, man. Did I say I was going to give anybody your number?"

"Well, don't," Bunting said. He felt as though he had been struck by a bolt of lightning a second ago. He looked down at his hands and saw that they, and presumably the rest of his body, had turned a curious lobster-red flecked with white spots.

"You're going to piss me off, man, because you ought to know you can trust me. I'm not just some jerk, Bunting. I'm trying to do something nice for you."

Bunting stared furiously down at his keyboard.

"You're starting to piss me off," Herko said in a low, quiet voice.

"Okay, I trust you," Bunting said, and continued staring at his keyboard until Herko retreated into his own cubicle.

At the end of the day Bunting left the office quickly and took the staircase to avoid having to wait for the elevator. When he reached the ground floor, he sensed two elevators opening simultaneously off to his right, and hurried toward the door, dreading that someone would call out his name. Bunting spun through the door and walked as quickly as he could to the corner, where he turned off on a deeply shadowed crosstown street. He pulled his sunglasses from his pocket and put them on. Strangers moved past him, and even the Oriental rug outlets and Indian restaurants that lined the street seemed interchangeable and anonymous. His pace slowed. It came to him that, without consciously planning to do so, he was walking away from his bus stop. Bunting experienced every sensation of running away from something, but had no clear idea of what he was running from. It was all an illusion: there was nothing to run from. Herko? The idea was absurd. He certainly did not have to run from fuzzy, noisy Frank Herko.

Bunting ambled along, too tired to walk all the way back to his building but aware of some new dimension, an anticipatory expectancy, in his life that made it pleasant to walk along the crosstown street.

He crossed Broadway and kept walking, thinking that he might even try to figure out which subway

could take him uptown. Bunting had taken the subway only once, shortly after his arrival in New York,
and on the hot, crowded train he had felt in mortal
danger. Every inch of the walls had been filled with
lunatic scribbling; every other male on the subway
had looked like a mugger. But Frank Herko took the
subway in from Brooklyn every day. According to
the newspapers, all the subway graffiti had been removed. Bunting had lived in New York for a decade
without getting mugged, he walked all alone down
dark streets, the subway could not possibly seem so
threatening to him now. And it was much faster than
the bus.

Bunting passed the entrance to a subway station
just as he had these thoughts, and he paused to look
at it. Stairs led down to a smoky blackness filled with
noise: up the filthy steps floated a stench of zoo, of
other people's private parts.

Bunting twitched away like a cat and kept walking west, committed now to walking to Eighth Avenue. He suddenly felt nearly bad enough to hail a
cab and spend five dollars on the trip home. It had
come to him that Frank Herko and his friend Lindy
were going to set about making him go out on a date
with a girl named Marty, and that this must have
been the vague pleasure that had lightened his mood
only minutes ago.

Nothing was right about this, the whole idea
was nightmarishly grotesque.

46

But why did the idea of a date have to be grotesque? He was a well-dressed man with a steady job. His looks were okay—definitely on the okay side. Worse people had millions of dates. Above all, Veronica had given him a kind of history, a level of experience no other data clerk could claim. He had spent hundreds of hours talking to Veronica in restaurants, another hundred in airplanes. He had travelled to Switzerland and stayed in luxury hotel suites.

Bunting realized that if something happened in your mind, it had happened—you had a memory of it, you could talk about it. It changed you in the same way as an event in the world. In the long run, there was very little difference between events in the world and events in the mind, because one reality inhabited them both. He had been the lover of a sophisticated Swiss woman named Veronica, and he could certainly handle a date with a scruffy acquaintance of Frank Herko's. Named Marty.

In fact, he could see her. He could summon her up. Her name and her friendship with Frank evoked a short, dark-haired, undemanding girl who liked to have a good time. She would be passably pretty, wear short skirts and fuzzy sweaters, and go to a lot of movies. A passive, good-hearted quality would balance her occasional crudeness. He would appear patrician, aloof, ironic to her—a sophisticated older man.

He could take her out once, in some indeterminate future time. The differences between them would speak for themselves, and he and Marty would part with a mixture of regret and relief. It was this infinitely postponable scenario that had hovered about him with such delightful vagueness.

Bunting turned up Eighth Avenue smiling to himself. When he saw that he was walking past a drugstore he turned in and moved through the aisles until he came to a large display of baby bottles. Here, beside the three kinds of Evenflo and the Playtex, hung bottles he had never heard of—no sturdy Prentisses, but squat little blue bottles and bottles with patterns and flags and teddy bears, a whole new range of baby bottles made by a company named Ama. Bunting saw instantly that Ama was a wonderful company. They were located in Florida, and they had a sunny, inventive, Floridian sensibility. Bunting began scooping up the bottles, and ended by carrying an awkward armful to the counter.

"How many babies you *got?*" the young woman behind the register asked him.

"These are for a project," Bunting said.

"Like a collection?" she asked. Her head tilted prettily in the dusty light through the big plate-glass window on Eighth Avenue.

"Yes, like a collection," Bunting said. "Exactly." He smiled at her bushy hair and puzzling eyes.

Outside the drugstore, he moved to the curb and raised his hand for a cab. With the same heightened

sense of self that came when he bought his splen-
did suits, he rode back to his building in the ripped
backseat of a jouncing, smelly taxi, splurging another
fifteen cents every time the meter changed.

IV

THAT NIGHT HE ATE A MICROWAVED
Lean Cuisine dinner and divided his attention between the evening news on his television set and the
array of freshly washed bottles on both sides of it.
The news seemed outmoded and repetitious, the
bottles various and pristine. The news had happened
before, the same murders and explosions and decla-
rations and demonstrations had occurred yesterday
and the day before and the week and month before
that, but the bottles existed in present time, unprec-
edented and extraordinary. The news was routine,
the bottles possessed wonder. It was difficult for him
to take his eyes from them.

How many bottles, he wondered, would it take
to fill up his table? Or his bed?

For an instant, he saw his entire room fes-
tooned, engorged with cylindrical glass and plastic
bottles—blue bottles covering one wall, yellow ones
another, a curving path between bottles on the floor,
a smooth cushion of nippled bottles on his bed.
Bunting blinked and smiled as he chewed on turkey.
He sipped Spanish burgundy from one of the new
glass Evenflos.

When he had dumped the Lean Cuisine tray in
the garbage and dropped his silverware in the sink,
Bunting scrubbed out the bottle, rinsed the nipple,
and set them on his draining board. He put a kettle
of hot water on the stove, two teaspoons of instant

coffee in one of his new bottles, and added boiling water and cold milk before screwing on the nipple. He poured a generous slug of cognac into another new bottle, a squat, pink, friendly-looking little Ama, and took both bottles to his bed along with a pen and a pad of paper. Bunting pulled coffee, then cognac, into his mouth, and let the little pink Ama dangle from his mouth while he wrote.

Dear Mom and Dad,

There have been some changes that I ought to tell you about. For some time there have been difficulties between Veronica and me which I haven't told you about because I didn't want you to worry about me. I guess what it all boils down to is that I've been feeling you could say stultified by our relationship. This has been difficult for both of us, after all the time we've been together, but things are finally resolved, and Veronica and I are only distant friends now. Of course there has been some pain, but I felt that my freedom was worth that price.

Lately I have been seeing a girl named Carol, who is really great. I met her in an art gallery where she works, and we hit it off right away. Carol makes me feel loved and cared for, and I love her already, but I'm not going to make the mistake of tying myself down so soon after breaking up with Veronica, and I'm going out with two other great girls too. I'll tell you about them in the weeks to come.

Unfortunately, I still will not be able to come for Christmas, since New York is getting so expensive, and my rent just went up to an astronomical sum...

If nobody hears the tree falling down in the forest, does it make any sound?

Does the air hear?

When his letter was done, Bunting folded it into an envelope and set it aside to be mailed in the morning. It was two hours to bedtime. He removed his jacket, loosened his tie, and slipped off his shoes. He thought of Veronica, sitting on the edge of a bed on the east side of town. A Merlin phone on a long cord sat beside her. Veronica's eyes were dark and hard, and a deep vertical line between her harsh thick eyebrows cut into her forehead. Bunting noticed for the first time that her calves were skinny, and that the loose skin beneath her eyes was a shade darker than the rest of her face. Without his noticing it, Veronica had been getting old. She had been hardening and drying like something left out in the sun. It came to him that he had always been unsuitable for her, and that was why she had chosen him. In her personal life, she set up situations destined from the first to fail. He had spent years "with" Veronica, but he had never understood this before.

He had been an actor in a psychic drama, and he had done no more than to play his role.

It came to him that Veronica had deliberately introduced him to a way of life he could not afford by himself in order to deprive him of it later. If he had not broken off with her, she would have dropped him. Veronica was a poignant case. Those winks and flashes of leg in office meetings had simply been aspects of a larger plan unconsciously designed to leave him gasping with pain. Without Bunting, she would find someone else—an impoverished young poet, say—and do the whole thing all over again, dinner at the Blue Goose and first-class trips to Switzerland (Bunting had not told his parents about travelling first class), orchestra seats at Broadway plays, until what was twisted in her made her discard him.

Bunting felt sort of...awed. He knew someone like that.

He washed the Evenflo, refilled the pink little bottle with cognac, and picked up his novel and went back to bed to read. For a moment he squirmed around on top of his sheets, getting into the right position. He sucked cognac into his mouth, swallowed, and opened the book.

The lines of print swam up to meet him, and instantly he was on top of a quick little grey horse named Shorty, looking down the brown sweep of a hill toward a herd of grazing buffalo. An enormous, nearly cloudless sky hung above him; far ahead, so distant they were colorless and vague, a bumpy line of mountains rose up from the yellow plain. Shorty began to pick his way down the hill, and Bunting saw that he was wearing stained leather chaps over his trousers, a dark blue shirt, a sheepskin vest, and muddy brown boots with tarnished spurs. Two baby bottles had been inserted, nipple-down, into the holsters on his hips, and a rifle hung in a long sheath from the pommel of his saddle. Shorty's muscles moved beneath his legs, and a strong smell of horse came momentarily to Bunting, then was gone in a general wave of fresh, living odors from the whole scene before him. A powerful smell of grass dominated, stronger than the faint, tangy smell of the buffalo. From a long way off, Bunting smelled fresh water. Off to the east, someone was burning dried sod in a fireplace. The strength and clarity of these odors nearly knocked Bunting off his horse, and Shorty stopped moving and looked around at him with a large, liquid brown eye. Bunting smiled and prodded Shorty with his heels, the horse continued walking quietly down the hill, and the astonishing freshness of the air sifted around and through him. It was the normal air of this world, the air he knew.

Shorty reached the bottom of the hill and began moving slowly alongside the great herd of buffalo. He wanted to move into a gallop, to cut toward the buffalo and divide them, but Bunting pulled back on the reins. Shorty's hide quivered, and the short coarse hairs scratched against Bunting's chaps. It was important to proceed slowly and get into firing range before scattering the buffalo. A few of the massive bearded heads swung toward Bunting and Shorty as they plodded west toward the front of the herd. One of the females snorted and pushed her way toward the center of the herd, and the others grunted and moved aside to let her pass. Bunting slipped his rifle from its case, checked to be sure it was fully loaded, and held it across his lap. He stuffed six extra bullets in each pocket of the sheepskin vest.

Shorty was ambling away past the front of the herd now, something like fifty yards away from the nearest animals. A few more of the buffalo watched him. Their furry mouths drizzled onto the grass. When he passed out of their immediate field of vision, they did not turn their heads but went back to nuzzling the thick grass. Bunting kept moving until he was far past the front of the herd, and then cut Shorty back around in a wide circle behind them.

The herd moved very slightly apart: now the males had noticed him, and were watching to see what he would do. Bunting knew that if he got off the horse and stood in the sun for a few minutes the males would walk up to him and stand beside him and find on him the smell of every place he had ever been in his life. Then the ones who liked those smells would stay around him and the rest would wander off a little way. That was what buffalo did, and it was fine if you could stand their own smell.

Bunting cocked his rifle, and one big male raised his head and shook it, as if trying to get rid of a bad dream.

Bunting kept Shorty moving on a diagonal line toward the middle of the herd, and the buffalo began moving apart very slowly.

The big male who had been watching seemed to come all the way out of his dream, and started ambling toward him. Bunting was something like ten yards from the big male, and twenty yards from most of the rest of the herd. It wasn't too bad: it could have been better, but it would do.

Bunting raised his rifle and aimed it at the center of the big male's forehead. The buffalo instantly stopped moving and uttered a deep sound of alarm that made the entire herd ripple. A single electrical impulse seemed to pass through all the animals ranged out before Bunting. Bunting squeezed the trigger, and the rifle made a flat cracking sound that instantly spread to all parts of the long grassy plain, and the big male went down on his front knees and then collapsed onto his side.

The rest of the herd exploded. Buffalo ran toward the hill and scattered across the plain. Bunting kicked Shorty into action and rode into their midst, shooting as he went. Two others fell instantly, then a third around whose body Shorty wheeled. Two of the fastest buffalo had reached the hill, and Bunting aimed and fired and brought them down. He reloaded as a line of panicked buffalo swung away from the hill and bolted deeper into the meadow. The leader fell and rolled, and Shorty carried Bunting up alongside the second in line. Bunting shot the second buffalo in the eye, and it shuddered and fell. He swivelled in the saddle and brought down two more that were pounding toward the opposite end of the endless meadow.

By now the grass was spattered with blood, and the air had become thick with the screams of dying animals and the buzzing of flies. Bunting's own hands were spotted with blood, and long smears of blood covered his chaps. He fired until the rifle was empty, and then he reloaded and fired again as Shorty charged and separated the stampeding buffalo, and in the end he thought that only a few of the fastest animals had escaped. Dead and dying buffalo like huge sacks of dark brown wool lay all over the meadow, males and females. A few infant buffalo who had been trampled in the panic lay here and there in the tall grass.

Bunting swung himself off Shorty and went moving among the prone buffalo, slitting open the bellies of the dead. A great rush of purple and silver entrails fell out of the dead buffalo's body cavities, and Bunting's arms grew caked with drying blood. At last he came to a young female that was struggling to get onto its feet. He took one of the baby bottles from his holster, put the barrel behind the animal's ear, and pulled the trigger. The female jerked forward and slammed its dripping muzzle into the grass. Bunting sliced open its belly.

He skinned the female, then moved to another. He managed to skin four of the buffalo, a third of all he had killed, before it grew too dark to work. His arms and shoulders ached from tearing the thick flesh away from the animals' fatty hides. The entire meadow reeked of blood and death. Bunting built a small fire and unrolled his pack beside it and lay down to doze until morning.

Then the meadow and the night and the piles of dead animals slid away into nothingness, into white space, and Bunting's head jerked up. He was lying in his bed, and there was no fire, and for a moment he did not understand why he could not see the sky. A close, stuffy odor, the odor of himself and his room, surrounded him. Bunting looked back at the book and saw that he had reached the end of a chapter. He shook his head, rubbed his face, and took in that he was wearing a shirt, a tie, the trousers to a good suit.

More than three hours had passed since he had picked up *The Buffalo Hunter*. He had been reading, and what he had read was a single chapter of a novel by Luke Short. The chapter had seemed incomparably more real than his own life. Now Bunting regarded the book as though it were a bomb, a secret weapon—it had stolen him out of the world. While he had been in the book, he had been more purely alive than at any other time during the day.

Bunting could not keep himself from testing the book again. His mouth was dry, and his heart was thumping hard enough nearly to shake the bed. He picked up the book and sucked cognac, for courage, from the little pink bottle. The book opened in his hand to the words CHAPTER THREE. He looked down to the first line of print, saw the words "The sun awakened him…" and in an instant he was lying on a bed of thick grass beside a low, smoky fire. His horse whickered softly. The sun, already warm, slanted into his eyes and dazzled him, and he threw off his blanket and got to his feet. His hips ached. A thick mat of flies covered the heaps of entrails, dark blood glistened on the grass, and Bunting closed his eyes and *wrenched* himself out of the page and back into his own body. He was breathing hard. The world of the book still seemed to be present, just out of sight, calling to him.

Hurriedly he put the book on the seat of his chair and stood up. The room swayed twice, right to left, left to right, and Bunting put out his hand to steady himself. He had been lost inside the book for only a few hours, but now it felt like he had spent an entire night asleep in a bloody meadow, keeping uneasy watch over a slaughtered herd. He turned the book over so that its cover was facedown on the chair and carried the bottle to the counter. He refilled it with cognac and took two large swallows before screwing the nipple back on.

What had happened to him was both deeply disturbing and powerfully, seductively pleasurable. It was as if he had travelled backward in time, gone into a different body and a different life, and there lived at a pitch of responsiveness and openness not available to him in his real, daily life. In fact, it had felt far more real than his "real" life. Bunting began to tremble again, remembering the clarity and freshness of the air, the touch of Shorty's coarse hair against his legs, the way the big male buffalo had come slowly toward him as the others began to stir apart—in that world, everything had possessed consequence. No detail was wasted because every detail overflowed with meaning.

He sucked the cognac into his mouth, troubled by something else that had just occurred to him.

Bunting had read *The Buffalo Hunter* three or four times before—he had a small shelf of Western and mystery novels, and he read them over and over. What troubled him was that there was no slaughter of buffalo in *The Buffalo Hunter*. Bunting could remember—vaguely, without any particularity—a few scenes in which the hunter rode down buffalo and killed them, but none in which he massacred great numbers and waded through their bloody entrails.

Bunting let the bottle hang from the nipple in his teeth and looked around his cramped, disorderly little room. For a moment—less than that, for an almost imperceptible fraction of a second—his familiar squalor seemed almost to tremble with promise, like the lips of one on the verge of telling a story. Bunting had the sense of some unimaginable anticipation, and then it was gone, so quickly it barely had time to leave behind the trace of an astonished curiosity.

He wondered if he dared go back to *The Buffalo Hunter*, and then knew he could not resist it. He would give himself a few more hours reading, then pull himself out of the book and make sure he got enough sleep.

Bunting took off the rest of his clothes and hung up the excellent suit. He brushed his teeth and ran hot water over the dishes in the sink to discourage the roaches. Then he turned off the overhead light and the other lamp and got into bed. His heart was beating fast again: he trembled with an almost sexual anticipation: and he licked his lips and took the book off the crowded seat of the chair. He nestled into the sheets and folded his pillow. Then at last Bunting opened the book once again.

V

WHEN THE WHITE SPACES CAME HE
held himself in suspension as he turned the page
and in this way went without a break from waking
in the morning and skinning the buffalo and rig-
ging a sledge to drag them behind Shorty to selling them to a hide broker and being ambushed and
nearly killed for his money. Bunting was thrown in
jail and escaped, found Shorty tethered in a feedlot,
and spent two nights sleeping in the open. He got a
job as a ranch hand and overheard enough to learn
that the hide broker ran the town: after that Bunting shot a man in a gunfight, escaped arrest again,
stole his hides back from a locked warehouse, killed
two more men in a gunfight, faced down the crooked
broker, and was offered and refused the position of
town sheriff. He rode out of the town back toward
the freedom he needed, and two days later he was
looking again across a wide plain toward grazing
buffalo. Shorty began trotting toward them, moving
at an angle that would take him past the top of the
herd. Bunting patted the extra shells in the pockets
of his sheepskin vest and slowly drew the rifle from
its sheath. A muscle twitched in Shorty's flank. A
shaggy female buffalo cocked her head and regarded
Bunting without alarm. Something was coming to
an end, Bunting knew, some way of life, some or-
dained, flawless narrative of what it meant to be alive
at this moment. A cold breeze carried the strong

aroma of buffalo toward him, and the sheer beauty and rightness—a formal rightness, inescapable and exact—of who and where he was went through Bunting like music, and as he sailed off into the final, the most charged and pregnant white space he could no longer keep himself from weeping.

Bunting let the book fall from his hands, back in a shrunken and diminished world. He experienced a long moment of pure loss from which only tremendous hunger and certain physical urgencies imperfectly distracted him. He needed, with overpowering urgency, to get into the bathroom; his legs had fallen asleep, his neck ached, and his knees creaked with pain. When he finally sat down on the toilet he actually cried out—it was as if he had gone days without moving. He realized that he was incredibly thirsty, and as he sat, he forced his arms to move to the sink, take up the glass, fill it with water. He swallowed, and the water forced its way down his throat and into his chest, breaking passage for itself. The world of Shorty, the meadow of endless green, and the grazing buffalo were already swimming backward, like a long night's dream. He was left behind in this littler, less eloquent world.

He turned on his shower and stepped inside to soak away his pains.

When he dried himself off, he realized that he had no proper idea of the time. Nor was he really certain of what day it was. He remembered seeing grey darkness outside his windows, so presumably it would soon be time to go to work—Bunting always awakened at the same time every day, seven-thirty, and had no need of an alarm: but suppose that he had read very late into the night, and had managed to get drunk, as on the night of his birthday: had he really just finished reading the book? *Living in* the book, as it actually seemed? That would mean that he had not slept at all, though it seemed to Bunting that he'd had the *experience* of sleeping, in gullies and in a little jailhouse, in a bunkhouse and a tavern's back room, and beside a fire in a wide meadow with millions of pinpoint stars overhead.

He dressed in a fresh shirt, a glen plaid suit, and a pair of cracked, well-polished brown shoes. When he strapped on his watch, he saw that it was six-thirty. He had read all night long, or most of it: he supposed he must have slept now and then, and dreamed certain passages of the book. Hunger forced him out of his room as soon as he was dressed, although he was an hour early: Bunting supposed he could walk to work again and get there early enough to clean up everything from Monday. Now that he was no longer so stiff, his body and his mind both felt, beneath a lingering layer of tiredness like that after a session of strenuous exercise, refreshed and energetic.

The light in the corridor seemed darker than it should have been, and in the lobby two teenage boys who had stayed up all night sucking on crack pipes and plotting crimes shared a thin hand-rolled cigarette beside the dying fern. Bunting hurried past them to the street. It was surprisingly crowded. He had gone halfway to the diner before the fact of the crowd, the darkness, and the whole feeling of the city combined into the recognition that it was evening, not morning. An entire day had disappeared.

Outside the diner, he bought a paper, looked at the date, and found that it was even worse than that. It was Thursday, not Tuesday: he had not left his apartment—not even his bed—for two and a half days. For something like sixty hours he had lived inside a book.

Bunting went into the bright diner, and the man behind the cash register, who had seen him at least four mornings a week for the past ten years, gave him an odd, apprehensive look. For a second or two the counterman also seemed wary of him. Then the man recognized him, and his face relaxed. Bunting tried to smile, and realized that he was still showing the shock he had felt at the loss of those sixty hours. His smile felt like a mask.

Bunting ordered a feta cheese omelette and a cup of coffee, and the counterman turned away toward the coffee machine. Headlines and rows of black print at Bunting's elbow seemed to lift up from the surface of the folded newspaper and blare out at him; the whole dazzle of the restaurant surged and chimed, as if saying *Wait for it, wait for it*: but the counterman turned carrying a white cup brimming with black coffee, the ink sifted down into the paper, and the sense of promise and anticipation faded back into the general bright surface of things.

Bunting lifted the thick china cup. Its rim was chalky and abraded with use. He was at a counter where he had eaten a thousand meals; the people around him offered the combination of anonymity and familiarity that most represents safety in urban life; but Bunting wanted overwhelmingly to be in his crowded little room, flat on his unmade bed, with the nipple of a baby bottle clamped between his teeth and a book open in his hands. If there was a promised land—a Promised Land—he had lived in it from Monday night to Thursday evening.

He was still in shock, and still frightened by the intensity of what had happened to him, but he knew more than anything else that he wanted to go back there.

When his omelette came it was overcooked and too salty, but Bunting bolted it down so quickly he scarcely tasted it. "You were hungry," the counterman said, and gave him his check without coming any nearer than he had to.

Bunting came out of the restaurant into what at first looked like an utter darkness punctuated here and there by street lamps and the headlights of the cars streaming down upper Broadway. Red lights flashed off and on. A massive policeman motioned Bunting aside, away from some commotion in the middle of the sidewalk. Bunting glanced past him and saw a body curled on the pavement, another man lying almost serenely prone with his hands stapled into handcuffs. A sheet of smooth black liquid lay across half the sidewalk. The policeman moved toward him, and Bunting hurried away.

More shocks, more disturbance—savage, pale faces came out of the dark, and cars sizzled past, honking. The red of the traffic lights burned into his eyes. All about him were creatures of another species, more animal, more instinctual, more brutal than he. They walked past him, unnoticing, flaring their lips and showing their teeth. He heard steps behind him and imagined his own body limp on the pockmarked concrete, his empty wallet tossed into the pool of his blood. The footsteps accelerated, and a white frozen panic filled Bunting's body. He stepped sideways, and a hand fell on his shoulder.

Bunting jumped, and a deep voice said, "Just hold it, will you?"

Bunting looked over his shoulder at a wide brutal face filled with black dots—little holes full of darkness—and a black moustache. He nearly fainted.

"I just wanted to ask some questions, sir."

Bunting took in the uniform at the same time as he saw the amusement on the policeman's face.

"You came out of the diner, didn't you, sir?"

Bunting nodded.

"Did you see what happened?"

"What?"

"The shooting, sir. Did you see a shooting?"

Bunting was trembling. "I saw—" He stopped talking, having become aware that he had intended to say *I saw myself shoot a man out west in a gunfight.* He looked wildly back toward the diner. A dozen policemen stood around a roped-off area of the sidewalk, and red lights flashed and spun. "I really didn't see anything at all. I barely saw—" He gestured toward the confusion.

The man nodded wearily and folded his notebook with a contemptuous, disbelieving snap. "Yeah," he said. "You have a good night, sir."

"I didn't see—I didn't—"

The policeman had already turned away.

On Bunting's side of the avenue, the lobby of his bank offered access to their rows of cash machines; across it, the drugstore's windows blared out light through a display of stuffed cartoon characters. A cardboard cut-out of a girl in a bathing suit held a camera. Bunting watched the policeman go back to his colleagues. Before they could begin talking about him, he ducked into the bank and removed a hundred dollars from his checking account.

When he came out again, he went to the corner, crossed the street without looking at the police cars lined up in front of the diner, and went into the drugstore. There he bought five tubes of epoxy glue and ninety dollars' worth of baby bottles and nipples, enough to fill a large box. He carried this awkwardly back to his building, peering over the top to see where he was going.

Bunting had to set down the box to push his button in the elevator, and again to let himself into his apartment. When he was finally safe inside his room, with the police bolt pushed back in front of the door, his lights on, and a colorful little Ama filled with vodka in his hand, he felt his true self returning to him, ragged and shredded from his nightmare on the streets. Except for the curious tingle of anticipation that had come to him in the diner, everything since being driven from his room by hunger had been like being attacked and beaten. Bunting could not even remember buying all the bottles and nipples, which had taken place in a tense, driven flurry.

Bunting began unpacking the baby bottles from the giant box, now and then stopping to suck cold Popov from the Ama. When he got to sixty-five, he saw that he was only one layer from the bottom, and was immediately sorry that he had not taken another hundred from the cash machine. He was going to need at least twice as many bottles to fulfil his plan, unless he spaced them out. He did not want to space them out, he wanted a nice tight look. A nice tight look was essential: a kind of *blanketing* effect.

Bunting thought he would try to do as much this night as he could with what he had, then get more money from the bank tomorrow evening and see how far another seventy or eighty bottles got him. When he was done tonight, he would read some more—not *The Buffalo Hunter* again, but some other novel, to see if the same incredible state of grace, like the ultimate movie, would come to him.

Bunting did not understand how, but what he wanted to do with all the new baby bottles was tied to what had happened to him when he read the Luke Short novel. It had to do with...with *inwardness.* That was as close as he could come to defining the connection. They led him *inward*, and inward was where everything important lay. He felt that though his entire way of life could be seen as a demonstration of this principle, he had never really understood it before—never seen it clearly. And he thought that this insight must have been what he felt coming toward him at the coffee shop: what mattered about his life took place entirely in this room.

When all the bottles were out of the box, Bunting began slicing open the packages of nipples and attaching the nipples to the bottles. When this was done, he opened a tube of epoxy and put a few dots on the base of one of the bottles. Then he pressed the bottle to the corner of a blank wall and held it there until it stuck. At last he lowered his arm and stepped away. The pink-tipped bottle adhered to the wall and jutted out into the room like an illusion. It took Bunting's breath away. The bottle appeared to be on the point of shooting or dripping milk, juice, water, vodka, any sort of fluid onto anyone in front of it.

He dotted epoxy onto the base of another bottle and held it to the wall snugly alongside the first.

An hour and a half later, when he ran out of new bottles, more than a third of the wall was covered: perfectly aligned horizontal bottles and jutting nipples marched along its surface from the entrance to the kitchen alcove to the door frame. Bunting's arms ached from holding the bottles to the wall, but he wished that he could finish the wall and go on to another. Beautiful now, the wall would be even more beautiful when finished.

Bunting stretched and yawned and went to the sink to wash his hands. A number of roaches ambled into their hiding places, and Bunting decided to wash the stacked dishes and glasses before the roaches started crowding each other out of the sink. He had his hands deep in soapy water when a thought disquieted him: he had not thought about the loss of all Tuesday, all Wednesday, and most of Thursday since buying the box of nipples and bottles, but what if his radical redecoration of his apartment was no more than a reaction to that loss?

But that was the viewpoint of another kind of mind. The world in which he went to work and came home was the world of public life. In that world, according to people like his father and Frank Herko, one "counted," "amounted to something," or did not. For a dizzy second, Bunting imagined himself entirely renouncing this worthless, superficial world to become a Magellan of the interior.

At that moment the telephone rang. Bunting dried his hands on the greasy dish towel, picked up the phone, and heard his father pronounce his name as if he were grinding it to powder. Bunting's heart stopped. The world had heard him. This unnerving impression was strong enough to keep him from taking in the meaning of his father's first few sentences.

"She fell down again?" he finally said.

"Yeah, something wrong with your ears? I just *said* that."

"Did she hurt herself?"

"About the same as before," his father said. "Like I say, I just thought you ought to know about stuff like this, when it happens."

"Well, is she bruised? Is her knee injured?"

"No, she mainly fell on her face this time, but her knee's just the same. She wears that big bandage on it, you know, probably kept her from busting the knee all up."

"What's making her fall down?" Bunting asked. "What does the doctor say?"

"I don't know, he don't say much at all. We're taking her in for some tests Friday, probably find out something then."

"Can I talk to her?"

"Nah, she's down in the basement, washing clothes. That's why I could call—she didn't even want me to tell you about what happened. She's on this washing thing now, she does the wash two, three times a day. Once I caught her going downstairs with a dish towel, she was going to put it in the machine."

Bunting glanced at his own filthy dish towel. "Why does she—what is she trying to—?"

"She forgets," his father said. "That's it, pure and simple. She forgets."

"Should I come out there? Is there anything I could do?"

"You made it pretty clear you *couldn't* come here, Bobby. We got your letter, you know, about Veronica and Carol and the rent and everything else. You tell us you got a busy social life, you tell us you got a steady job but you don't have much extra money. That's your life. And what could you do anyhow?"

Bunting said, "Not much, I guess," feeling stung and dismissed by this summary.

"Nothing," his father said. "I can do everything that has to be done. If she does the wash twice a day, what's the big deal? That's okay with me. We got the doctor appointment Friday, that's all set. And what's he going to say? Take it easy, that's what, it'll cost us thirty-five bucks to hear this guy telling your mother to take it easy. So as far as we know yet, everything's basically okay. I just wanted to keep you up to date. Glad I caught you in."

"Oh, sure. Me, too."

"'Cause you must be out a lot these days, huh? You must get out even more than you used to, right?"

"I'm not sure," Bunting said.

"I never could get a straight answer out of you, Bobby," his father said. "Sometimes I wonder if you know how to give one. I been calling you for two days, and all you say is *I'm not sure.* Anyhow, keep in touch."

Bunting promised to keep in touch, and his father cleared his throat and hung up without actually saying good-bye.

Bunting sat staring at the telephone receiver for a long time, barely conscious of what he was doing, not thinking and not aware of not thinking. He could not remember what he had been doing before the telephone rang: he had been puffed up with self -importance, it seemed to him now, as inflated as a bullfrog. He pictured his mother trotting down the basement stairs toward the washing machine with a single dish towel in her hands. Her bruised face was knotted with worry, and a thick white pad had been clamped to her knee with a tightly rolled Ace bandage. She looked as driven as if she held a dying baby. He saw her drop the cloth into the washing machine, pour in a cup of Oxydol, close the lid, and punch the starting button. Then what did she do? Nod and walk away, satisfied that one tiny scrap of the universe had been nailed into place? Go upstairs and wander around in search of another dishcloth, a single sock, a handkerchief?

Did she fall down inside the house?

He set the receiver back in its cradle and stood up. Before he knew he intended to go there, he was across the room and in front of the rows of bottles. He spread his arms and leaned forward. Rubber nipples pressed against his forehead, his closed eyes, cheeks, shoulders, and chest. He turned his face sideways, spread his arms, and moved in tighter. It was something like lying on a fakir's bed of nails, he thought. It was pretty good. It wasn't bad at all. He liked it. The nipples were harder than he had expected, but not painfully hard. Not a single bottle moved—the epoxy clamped them to the wall. Nothing would get these bottles off the wall, short of a blowtorch or a cold chisel. Bunting was slightly in awe of what he had done. He sighed. *She forgets. That's it, pure and simple.* Tough little nipples pressed lightly against the palms of his hands. He began to feel better. His father's voice and the image of his mother darting downstairs to drop a single cloth into the washing machine receded to a safe distance. He straightened up and passed his palms over the rows of nipples, which flattened against his skin and then bounced back into position. Tomorrow he would have to go to the bank and withdraw more money. Another hundred to hundred and fifty would finish the wall.

He couldn't go to Battle Creek, anyhow: it would be a waste of time. His mother already had an appointment with a doctor.

He backed away from the wall. The image of the fakir's bed resurfaced in his mind: nails, blood leaking from punctured skin. He shook it off by taking a long drink from the Ama. The vodka burned all the way down his throat. Bunting realized that he was slightly drunk.

He could do no more tonight; his arms and shoulders still ached from gluing the bottles onto the wall; he would tip just a little more vodka into the Ama—another inch, for an hour's reading—and get into bed. He had to go to work tomorrow.

As he folded and hung up the day's clothes, Bunting looked over his row of books, wondering if the *Buffalo Hunter* experience would ever be given to him again, afraid that reading might just be reading again.

On the other hand, he was also afraid that it might not be. Did he want to jump down the rabbit hole every time he opened a book?

Bunting had been groping toward the clothes rail with the suit hanger in his hand while looking down at his row of books, and finally he leaned into his closet and put the hook on the rail so that he could really inspect the books. There were thirty or forty, all of them paperbacks and all at least five or six years old. Some of them dated to his first days in New York. All the paperbacks had curling covers, cracked spines, and pulpy pages that looked as if they had been dunked in a bathtub. Slightly more than half of these were Westerns, many of these taken from Battle Creek. Most of the others were mysteries. He finally selected one of these, *The Lady in the Lake*, by Raymond Chandler.

It would be a relatively safe book to see from the inside—it wasn't one of the books where Philip Marlowe got beaten up, shot full of drugs, or locked away in a mental hospital. As importantly, he had read it last year and remembered it fairly well. He would be able to see if any important details changed once he got inside the book.

Bunting carefully brushed his teeth and washed his face. He peered through his blinds and looked out at the dingy brownstones, wondering if any of the people who lived behind those lighted windows had ever felt anything like his fearful and impatient expectancy.

Bunting checked the level in his bottle and turned off his other lamp. Then he switched it on again and ducked into his closet to find an alarm clock he had brought with him from Michigan but never needed. Bunting extracted the clock from a bag behind his shoes, set it to the proper time, shoved various things off the bedside chair to make room for it, and wound it up. After he set the alarm for seven-thirty he switched off the light near the sink. Now the only light burning in his room was the reading lamp at the head of the bed. Bunting turned down his covers with an almost formal sense of ceremony and got into bed. He folded his pillow in half and wedged it behind his head. He licked his lips and opened *The Lady in the Lake* to the first chapter. Blood pounded in his temples, his fingertips, and at the back of his head. The first sentence swam up at him, and he was gone.

VI

NEARLY EVERYTHING WAS DIFFERENT,
the cloudy air, the loud ringing sounds, the sense of
a wide heartbreak, his taller, more detached self, and
one of the greatest differences was that this time he
had a vast historical memory, comprehensive and in-
vestigatory—he knew that the city around him was
changing, that its air was far more poisoned than the
beautiful clean air of the meadow where the buffalo
grazed but much cleaner than the air of New York
City forty-five years hence: some aspect of himself
was familiar with a future in which violence, ignorance, and greed had finally won the battle. He was
walking through downtown Los Angeles, and men
were tearing up a rubber sidewalk at Sixth and Olive.
The world beat in on him, its sharp particulars urged
him toward knowledge, and as he entered a building and was instantly in a seventh-floor office his eye
both acknowledged and deflected that knowledge by
assessing the constant stream of details—double-
plate glass doors bound in platinum, Chinese rugs,
a glass display case with tiers of creams and soaps
and perfumes in fancy boxes. A man named Kingsley wanted him to find his mother. Kingsley was a
troubled man of six-two, elegant in a chalk-striped
grey flannel suit, and he moved around his office a lot
as he talked. His mother and his stepfather had been
in their cabin up in the mountains at Puma Point for
most of the summer, and then had suddenly stopped

communicating.

"Do you think they left the cabin?" Bunting asked.

Kingsley nodded.

"What have you done about it?"

"Nothing. Not a thing. I haven't even been up there." Kingsley waited for Bunting to ask why, and Bunting could smell the man's anger and impatience. He was like a cocked and loaded gun.

"Why?" he asked.

Kingsley opened a desk drawer and took out a telegraph form. He passed it over, and Bunting unfolded it under Kingsley's smouldering gaze. The wire had been sent to Derace Kingsley at a Beverly Hills address and said: I AM DIVORCING CHRIS STOP MUST GET AWAY FROM HIM AND THIS AWFUL LIFE STOP PROBABLY FOR GOOD STOP GOOD LUCK MOTHER.

When Bunting looked up Kingsley was handing him an eight-by-ten glossy photograph of a couple in bathing suits sitting on a beach beneath a sun umbrella. The woman was a slim blonde in her sixties, smiling and still attractive. She looked like a good-looking widow on a cruise. The man was a handsome brainless animal with a dark tan, sleek black hair, and strong shoulders and legs.

"My mother," Kingsley said. "Crystal. And Chris Lavery. Former playmate. He's my stepfather."

"Playmate?" Bunting asked.

"To a lot of rich women. My mother was just the one who married him. He's a no-good son of a bitch, and there's never been any love lost between us."

Bunting asked if Lavery were at the cabin.

"He wouldn't stay a minute if my mother went away. There isn't even a telephone. He and my mother have a house in Bay City. Let me give you the address." He scribbled on a stiff sheet of stationery from the top of his desk—*Derace Kingsley, Gillerlain Company*—and folded the card in half and handed it to Bunting like a state secret.

"Were you surprised that your mother wanted out of the marriage?"

Kingsley considered the question while he took a panatela out of a copper and mahogany box and beheaded it with a silver guillotine. He took his time about lighting it. "I was surprised when she wanted *in*, but I wasn't surprised when she wanted to dump him. My mother has her own money, a lot of it, from her family's oil leases, and she always did as she pleased. I never thought her marriage to Chris Lavery would last. But I got that wire three weeks ago, and I thought I'd hear from her long before now. Two days ago a hotel in San Bernardino called me to say that my mother's Packard Clipper was unclaimed in their garage. It's been there for better than two weeks. I figured she was out of the state, and sent them a check to hold the car. Yesterday I ran into Chris Lavery in front of the Athletic Club and he acted as if nothing had happened—when I confronted him with what I knew, he denied everything and said that as far as he knew, she was enjoying herself up at the cabin."

"So that's where she is," Bunting said.

"That bastard would lie just for the fun of it. But there's another angle here. My mother has had trouble with the police occasionally." He looked genuinely uncomfortable now, and Bunting helped him out. "The police?"

"She helps herself to things from stores. Especially when she's had too many martinis at lunch. We've had some pretty nasty scenes in managers' offices. So far nobody's filed charges, but if something happened in a strange city where nobody knew her—" He lifted his hands and let them fall back onto the desk.

"Wouldn't she call you, if she got into trouble?"

"She might call Chris first," Kingsley admitted. "Or she might be too embarrassed to call anybody."

"Well, I think we can almost throw the shoplifting angle out of this," Bunting said. "If she'd left her husband and gotten into trouble, the police would be likely to get in touch with you."

Kingsley poured himself a drink to help himself with his worrying. "You're making me feel better."

"But a lot of other things could have happened. Maybe she ran away with some other man. Maybe she had a sudden loss of memory—maybe she fell down and hurt herself somewhere, and she can't remember her name or where she lives. Maybe she got into some jam we haven't thought of. Maybe she met foul play."

"Good God, don't say that," Kingsley said.

"You've got to consider it," Bunting told him. "All of it. You never know what's going to happen to a woman your mother's age. Plenty of them go off the rails, believe me—I've seen it again and again. They start washing dishcloths in the middle of the night. They fall down in parking lots and mess up their faces. They forget their own names."

Kingsley stared at him, horrified. He took another slug of his drink.

"I get a hundred dollars a day, and a hundred right now," Bunting said.

Bunting drove to an address in Bay City that Kingsley's secretary gave him. The bungalow where Kingsley's mother had lived with Chris Lavery lay on the edge of the 'V' forming the inner end of a deep canyon. It was built downward, and the front door was slightly below street level. Patio furniture stood on the roof. The bedrooms would be in the basement, and lowest of all, like the corner pocket on a pool table, was the garage. Korean moss edged the flat stones of the front walk. An iron knocker hung on the narrow door below a metal grille.

Bunting pounded the knocker against the door. When nothing happened, he pushed the bell. Then he hammered on the knocker again. No one came to the door. He walked around the side of the house and lifted the garage door to eye level. A car with white sidewalls was inside the garage. He went back to the front door.

Bunting pushed the bell and banged on the door, thinking that Chris Lavery might have been sleeping off a hangover. When there was still no response, Bunting twisted back and forth in front of the door, uncertain of his next step. He would have to drive up to the lake, that was certain, but now he felt that he would drive all day and get nowhere—at Puma Point there would be another empty building, and he would stand at another door, knocking and ringing, and nobody would ever let him in. He would stand outside in the dark, banging on a locked door.

How had he become a detective? What had made him do it? *That* was the mystery, it seemed to him, not the whereabouts of some rich idiot who had married a playboy. He touched the little pink Ama bottle in his shoulder holster, for comfort.

Bunting stepped off the porch and walked back around the side of the house to the garage. He swung up the door, went inside, and pulled the door down behind him. The car with whitewalls was a big roadster convertible that would gulp down gasoline like it was vodka and looked as if it could hit a hundred and twenty on the highway. Bunting realized that if he had the key, he could turn on the ignition, lean back in the seat, stick his good old bottle in his mouth, and take the long, long ride. He could make the long good-bye, the one you never came back from.

But he did not have the key to the roadster, and even if he did, he had a business card with a Tommy Gun in the corner; he had to detect. At the back of the garage was a plywood door leading into the house. The door was locked with something the builder had bought at a five and dime, and Bunting kicked at the door until it broke open. Wooden splinters and tiny pieces of metal sprayed into the hallway.

Bunting stepped inside. His heart was beating fast, and he thought, with sudden clarity: *This is why I'm a detective.* It was not just the excitement, it was the sense of imminent discovery. The whole house lay above him like a beating heart, and he was in a passage *inside* that heart.

The hushed warm smell of late morning in a closed house came to him, along with the odor of Vat 69. Bunting began moving down the hall. He glanced into a guest bedroom with drawn blinds. At the end of the hall he stepped into an elaborately furnished bedroom where a crystal greyhound stood on a smeary mirror-top table. Two pillows lay side by side on the unmade bed, and a pink towel with lipstick smears hung over the side of the wastebasket. Red lipstick smears lay like slashes across one of the pillows. Some foul, emphatic perfume hung in the air.

Bunting turned to the bathroom door and put his hand on the knob.

No, he did not want to look in the bathroom—
he suddenly realized that he wanted to be anyplace
at all, a Sumatran jungle, a polar ice cap, rather than
where he was. The lipstick stain on the towel dripped
steadily onto the carpet, turning it into a squashy red
mush. He looked at the bed, and saw that the second
pillow glistened with red that had leaked onto the
sheet.

No, he said inside himself, please no, not again.
One of them is in there, or both of them are in there,
and it'll look like a butcher shop, you don't want, you
can't, it's too much…

He turned the knob and opened the door. His
eyes were nearly closed. Drools and sprays of blood
covered the floor. A fine spattering of blood misted
the shower curtain.

It's only Bunting, finding another body. Body-a-
day Bunting, they call him.

He walked through the blood and pushed back
the shower curtain.

The tub was empty—only a thick layer of blood
lay on the bottom of the tub, slowly oozing down
the drain.

The hideous clanging of a bell came to him
through the bathroom windows. A white space in
the air filled with the sound of the bell. Bunting
clapped his hands to his ears. His neck hurt, and his
back ached. He turned to flee the bathroom, but the
bathroom had disappeared into empty white space.
His legs could not move. Pain encased his body like

St. Elmo's fire, and he groaned aloud and closed his eyes and opened them to the unbearable enclosure of his room and the shrieking clock.

For a moment he knew that the walls of this room were splashed with someone's blood, and he dropped the book and scuttled off the bed, gasping with pain and terror. His legs folded away, and he fell full-length on the floor. His legs cried out, his entire body cried out. He could not move. He began writhing toward the door, moaning, and stopped only when he realized that he was back in his room. He lay on his carpet, panting, until the blood had returned to his legs enough for him to stand up and go into the bathroom. He had a difficult moment when he had to pull back the shower curtain, but none of the numerous stains on the porcelain and the wall tiles were red, and hot water soon brought him back into his daily life.

VII

THE NEXT SIGNIFICANT EVENT IN
Bunting's life followed the strange experience just
described as if it had been rooted in or inspired by
it, and began shortly after he left his building to go
to work. He had a slight headache, and his hands
trembled: it had seemed to him while tying his necktie that his face had subtly altered in a way that the
discolored bags under his eyes did not entirely account for. His cheeks looked sunken, and his skin
was an almost unnatural white. He supposed that he
had not slept at all. He looked as if he were still staring at the bloody bathtub.

A layer of skin had been peeled away from him.
All the colors and noises on the street seemed brighter
and louder, everything seemed several notches more
alive—the cars streaming down the avenue, the men
and women rushing along the sidewalk, the ragged
bums holding their paper bags. Even the little pieces
of grit and paper whirled by the wind seemed like
messages. Although he was never truly conscious of
this, Bunting usually tried to take in as little as possible on his way to work. He thought of himself as
in a transparent bubble which protected him from
unnecessary pain and distraction. That was how
you lived in New York City—you moved around inside an envelope of tough resistant varnish. A crew
of men in orange hard hats and jackets were taking
up the concrete sidewalk down the block from his

building, and the sound of a jackhammer pounded in Bunting's ears. For a second the world wobbled around him, and he was back in the Los Angeles of forty years before, on his way to see a man named Derace Kingsley. He shuddered, then remembered: in the first paragraph of *The Lady in the Lake*, he had seen workmen taking up a rubber sidewalk.

For a second the clouds parted, and bright sunlight fell upon Bunting and everything before him. Then the air went dark.

The sound of the jackhammers abruptly ceased, and the workmen behind Bunting began shouting indistinct, urgent words. They had found something under the sidewalk, and because Bunting had to get away from what they had found, he took one quick step toward his bus stop. Then a wall of water smashed against his head—without any warning, a thick drenching rainfall had soaked his clothes, his hair, and everything and everybody about him. The air turned black in an instant, and a loud roll of thunder, followed immediately by a crack of lightning that illuminated the frozen street, obliterated the shouts of the workmen. The lightning turned the world white for a brief electric moment: Bunting could not move. His suit was a wet rag, and his hair streamed down the sides of his face. The sudden rainfall and the lightning that illuminated the water bouncing crazily off the roof of the bus shelter threw Bunting right out of his frame. What had been promised for days had finally arrived. His eyes had been washed clean of habit, and he *saw*.

People thrust past him to get into doorways and beneath the roof of the bus shelter, but he neither could, nor wanted to, move. It was as if all of life had gloriously opened itself before him. If he could have moved, he would have fallen to his knees with thanks. For long, long seconds after the lightning faded, everything blazed and burned with life. Being streamed from every particle of the world—wood, metal, glass, or flesh. Cars, fire hydrants, the concrete and crushed stones of the road, each individual raindrop, all contained the same living substance that Bunting himself contained—and this was what was significant about himself and them. If Bunting had been religious, he would have felt that he had been given a direct, unmediated vision of God: since he was not, his experience was of the sacredness of the world itself.

All of this took place in a few seconds, but those seconds were out of time altogether. When the experience began to fade, and Bunting began to slip out of eternity back into time, he wiped the mixture of rain and tears from his face and started to move toward the bus shelter. It seemed that he too had overflowed. He moved beneath the roof of the bus shelter. Several people were looking at him oddly. He wondered what his face looked like—it seemed to him that he might be glowing. The bus appeared in the rainy darkness up the avenue, lurching and rolling through the potholes like an ocean liner. What had happened to him—what he was already beginning to think of as his "experience"—was similar, he realized, to what he felt when he tumbled into *The Buffalo Hunter*.

He sighed loudly and wiped his eyes. The people nearest him moved away.

VIII

HE ARRIVED AT DATACOMCORP soaked and irritable, not knowing why. He wanted to push people who got in his way, to yell at anyone who slowed him down. He blamed this feeling on having to arrive at the office in wet clothes. The truth was that discomfort caused only the smallest part of his anger. Bunting felt as if he had been forced into an enclosure too small for him: he had left a mansion and returned to a hovel. The glimpse of the mansion made the hovel unendurable.

He came stamping out of the elevator and scowled at the receptionist. As soon as he was inside his cubicle, he ripped off his suit jacket and threw it at a chair. He yanked down his tie and rubbed his neck and forehead with his damp handkerchief. In a dull, ignorant fury he banged his fist against his computer's on switch and began punching in data. If Bunting had been in a better mood, his natural caution would have protected him from the mistake he made after Frank Herko appeared in his cubicle. As it was, he didn't have a chance—foolhardy anger spoke for him.

"The Great Lover returns at last," Herko said.

"Leave me alone," said Bunting.

"Bunting the Infallible shows up still drunk after partying with his lovely bimbo, misses work for two days, doesn't answer his phone, shows up half-drowned—"

"Get out, Frank," Bunting said.

"—and madder than a stuck bull, probably suffering from flu if not your actual pneumonia—"

Bunting sneezed.

"—and expects the only person who really understands him to shut up and leave him alone. God, you're *soaked*. Don't you have any sense? Hold on, I'll be right back."

Bunting growled. Herko slipped out of the cubicle, and a minute later returned with both hands full of wadded, brown paper napkins from the dispenser in the men's room. "Dry yourself off, will you?"

Bunting snarled and swabbed his face with some of the napkins. He scrubbed napkins in his hair, unbuttoned his shirt and rubbed napkins over his damp chest.

"So what were you doing?" Herko asked. "Coming down with double pneumonia?"

Herko was a hysterical fool. Also, he thought he owned Bunting. Bunting did not feel ownable. "Thanks for the napkins," he said. "Now get out of here."

Herko threw up his hands. "I just wanted to tell you that I set up your date with Marty for tonight. I suppose that's still all right, or do you want to kill me for that, too?"

Around Bunting the world went white. His blood stopped moving in his veins. "You set up my date?"

"Well, Marty was eager to meet you. Eight o'clock, at the bar at One Fifth Avenue. Then you're in the Village, you can go to eat at a million places right around there." Herko leaned forward to peer at Bunting's face. "What's the matter? You sick again? Maybe you should go home."

Bunting whirled to face his computer. "I'm okay. Will you get the hell out of here?"

"Jesus," Herko said. "How about some thanks?"

"Don't do me any more favors, okay?" Bunting did not take his eyes from his screen, and Herko retreated.

Late in the afternoon, Bunting put his head around the door of his friend's cubicle. Herko glanced up, frowning. "I'm sorry," Bunting said. "I was in a bad mood this morning. I know I was rude, and I want to apologize."

"Okay," Herko said. "That's all right." He was still a little stiff and wounded. "It's okay about the date, right?"

"Well," Bunting said, and saw Herko's face tighten. "No, it's fine. Sure. That's great. Thanks."

"You'll love the bar," Herko said. "And then you're right down there in the Village. Million restaurants, all around you."

Bunting had never been in Greenwich Village, and knew only of the restaurants, many of them invented, to which he had taken Veronica. Then something else occurred to him.

"You like Raymond Chandler, don't you?" he asked, having remembered an earlier conversation.

"Ray is my man, my *main* man."

"Do you remember that part in *The Lady in the Lake* where Marlowe first goes to Chris Lavery's house?"

Herko nodded, instantly in a better mood.

"What does he find?"

"He finds Chris Lavery."

"Alive?"

"Well, how else could he talk to him?"

"He doesn't find a lot of blood splashed all over the bathroom, does he?"

"What's happening to you?" Herko asked. "You starting to put the great literature of our time through a mental shredder, or what?"

"Or what," Bunting said, though it seemed that he had certainly shuffled, if not actually shredded, the pages he had read. He backed out of the cubicle and disappeared into his own.

Herko sat quiet with surprise for a moment, then yelled, "Long fangs! Long, long fangs! Bunting's gone a-hunting!" He howled like a wolf.

Some of the ladies giggled, and one of them said that he shouldn't tease. Herko started laughing big chesty barrelhouse laughs.

Bunting sat behind his computer, trying to force himself to concentrate on his work. Herko gasped for breath, then went on rolling out laughter. The bubble of noise about him suddenly evoked the image of the workmen who had exclaimed, an instant before the sudden storm, over the hole they had made in the sidewalk: they had found a dead man in that hole.

Bunting knew this with a sudden and absolute certainty. The men working on the sidewalk had looked down into that hole and seen a rotting corpse, or a heap of bones and a skull in a dusty suit, or a body in some stage between these two. Bunting saw the open mouth, the matted hair, the staring eyes and the writhing maggots. He tried to wrench himself back into the present, where his own living body sat in a damp shirt before a computer terminal filled with what for the moment looked alarmingly like gibberish.

DATATRAX 30 CARTONS MONMOUTH NJ BLUE CODE RED CODE

Jesus stepped past the rock at the mouth of the tomb, spread his arms wide, and sailed off in his dusty white robe into a flawless blue sky.

That's my body, he thought. *My* body.

Something the size of a walnut rattled in his stomach, grew to the size of an apple, then developed a point that lengthened into a needle. Bunting held his hands to his stomach and rushed out of the Data Entry room into the corridor. He banged through the men's room door and entered a toilet stall not much smaller than his cubicle. He pressed his necktie to his chest to avoid spattering, bent over, and vomited.

In the middle of the afternoon, Bunting looked up from his screen and saw the flash of a green dress moving past the door of his cubicle. The color was a dark flat green that both stood out from the office's pale walls and harmonized with them, and for an instant it seemed to float toward Bunting, who had been daydreaming about nothing in particular. The flat green jumped into sharp focus; then it was gone. The air the woman had filled hummed with her absence, and suddenly all the world Bunting could see promised to overflow with sacred and eternal being, as it had that morning. Bunting braced himself and fought the rising sense of expectancy—he did not know why, but he had to resist. The world instantly lost the feeling of trembling anticipation that had filled it a moment before: every detail fell back into itself. Jesus went back into his cave and rolled the rock back across the entrance. The workmen standing in the rain looked down into an empty hole. Bunting was still alive, or still dead. He had been saved. The tree had fallen in the deep forest, and no one had heard it, so it still stood.

That night Bunting again set his alarm and went back into *The Lady in the Lake*. He was driving into the mountains, and once he got to a place called Bubbling Springs, the air grew cool. Canoes and rowboats went back and forth on Puma Lake, and speedboats filled with squealing girls zipped past, leaving wide foamy wakes. Bunting drove through meadows dotted with white irises and purple lupines. He turned off at a sign for Little Fawn Lake and crawled past granite rocks. He drove past a waterfall and through a maze of black oak trees. Now everything about him sang with meaning, and he was alive within this meaning, as alive as he was supposed to be, equal to the significance of every detail within the landscape. A woodpecker peered around a tree trunk, an oval lake curled at the bottom of a valley, a small bark-covered cabin stood against a stand of oaks. This information came toward and into him in a steady stream, every glowing feather and shining outcropping of rock and inch of wood overflowing with its portion of being, and Bunting, the eye around which this speaking world cohered, moved through this stream of information undeflected and undisturbed.

He got out of his car and pounded on the cabin door, and a man named Bill Chess came limping into view. Bunting gave Bill Chess a drink from a pint of rye in his pocket and they sat on a flat rock and talked. Bill Chess's wife had left him, and his mother had died. He was lonely in the mountains. He didn't know anything about Derace Kingsley's mother. Eventually, they went up the heavy wooden steps to Kingsley's cabin and Chess unlocked the door and they went inside to the hushed warmth. Bunting's heart was breaking. Everything he saw looked like a postcard from a world without grief. The floors were plain and the beds were neat. Bill Chess sat down on one of the cream-colored bedspreads while Bunting opened the door to the bathroom. The air was hot, and the stink of blood stopped him as soon as he stepped inside. Bunting moved to the shower curtain, knowing that what was left of Crystal Kingsley's body lay inside the tub. He held his breath and grasped the curtain. When he pushed it aside, Bill Chess cried out behind him. "Muriel! Sweet Christ, it's Muriel!" But there was no body in the tub, only a bloodstain hardening as it oozed toward the drain.

IX

AT SEVEN-THIRTY ON FRIDAY NIGHT,
Bunting sat at a table facing the entrance of One
Fifth Avenue, alternately checking his watch and
looking at the door. He had arrived fifteen minutes
before, dressed in one of his best suits, showered,
freshly shaved, black wingtips and teeth brushed,
his mouth tingling with Binaca. To get to the bar,
which was already crowded, you had to walk past
the tables, and Bunting planned to get a good look at
this woman before she saw him. After that he would
know what to do. The waitress came around, and
he ordered another vodka martini. Bunting thought
he felt comfortable. His heart was beating fast, and
his hands were sweaty, but that was okay, Bunting
thought—after all, this was his first date, his first
real date, since he had broken up with Veronica. In
another sense, one he did not wish to consider, this
was his first date in twenty years. Every couple of
minutes, he went to the men's room and splashed
water on his face. He fluffed up his hair and buffed
his shoes with paper towels. Then he went back to
his table and sipped his drink and watched the door.

He wished that he had thought of secreting an
Ama in one of his pockets. Even a loose nipple would
work: he could tuck it into his mouth whenever he
felt anxious. Or just keep it in his pocket!

Bunting shot his cuffs, ran a hand over his hair,
looked at his watch. He leaned on his elbows and

stared at the people in the bar. Most of them were younger than himself, and all of them were talking and laughing. He checked the door again. A young woman with black hair and round glasses had just entered, but it was still only twenty minutes to eight—far too early for Marty. He pulled out his handkerchief and wiped his forehead, wondering if he ought to go back into the bathroom and splash more water on his face. He felt a little bit hot. Still okay, but just a tad hot. He advised himself to think about all those times he had gone to fancy places with Veronica, and shoved his hands in his pockets and tried to remember the exact feelings of walking into Quaglino's beside his tall, executive girlfriend…

"Bob? Bob Bunting?" someone said in his ear, and he jumped forward as if he had been jabbed with a fork. His chest struck the table, and his glass wobbled. He stabbed out a hand to grasp the drink and knocked it over. Clear liquid spilled out and darkened the tablecloth. Two large olives rolled across the table, and one of them fell to the floor. Bunting uttered a short, mortifying shriek. The woman who had spoken to him was laughing. She placed a hand on his arm. He whirled around on his chair, bumping his elbow on the table's edge, and found the black-haired woman who had just entered the restaurant staring down at him with a quizzical alarm.

"After all that, I hope you are Bob Bunting," she said.

Bunting nodded. "I hope I am, too," he said. "I don't seem to be too sure, do I? But who are you? Do we know each other?"

"I'm Marty," she said. "Weren't you waiting for me?"

"Oh," he said, understanding everything at last. She was a short, round-faced young woman with a restless, energetic quality that made Bunting instantly feel tired. Her eyes were very blue and her lipstick was very red. At the moment she seemed to be inwardly laughing at him. "Excuse me, my goodness," he said, "yes, of course, how nice to meet you." He got to his feet and held out his hand.

She took it, not bothering to conceal her amusement. "You been here long?"

She had a strong New York accent.

"A little while," he confessed.

"You wanted to check me out, didn't you?"

"Well, no. Not really." He thought with longing of his room, his bed, his wall of bottles, and *The Lady in the Lake*. "How did you know who I was?"

"Frank described you, how else? He said you'd be dressed like a lawyer and that you looked a little shy. Do you want to have another drink here, now that I made you spill that one? I'll have one, too."

He took her coat to the checkroom, and when he returned he found a fresh martini at his place, a glass of white wine in front of Marty, and a clean tablecloth on the table. She was smiling at him. He could not decide if she was unusually pretty or just disconcerting. "You did get here early to check me out, didn't you?" she asked. "If you didn't like the way I looked, you could duck out when I went into the bar."

"I'd never do that."

"Why not? I would. Why do you think I got here so early? I wanted to check you out. Blind dates make me feel funny. Anyhow, I knew who you were right away, and you didn't look so bad. I was afraid you might be real gonzo, from what Frank said about you, but I knew that anybody as nervous as you couldn't really be gonzo."

"I'm not nervous," Bunting said.

"Then why did you go off like a bomb when I said your name?"

"You startled me."

"Well, I couldn't have startled you if you weren't nervous. It's okay. You never saw me before, either. So tell me the truth—if you saw me walk in the door, and if I didn't notice you, would you have cut out? Or would you have gone through with it?"

She raised her glass and sipped. Her eyes were so blue that the color had leaked into the whites, spreading a faint blue nimbus around the irises. He saw for the first time that she was wearing a black dress that fit her tightly, and that her eyebrows were firm black lines. She seemed exotic, almost mysterious, despite her forthright manner. She was, he realized, startlingly good-looking. Then he suddenly saw her naked, a vision of smooth white skin and large soft breasts.

"Oh," he said, "I would have gone through with it, of course."

"Why are you blushing? Your whole face just turned red."

He shrugged in an agony of embarrassment. He was certain that she knew what he had been thinking. He gulped at his drink.

"You're not exactly what I expected, Bob," she said in a very dry voice.

"Well, you're not quite what I expected, either," was all he could think to say. Unable to look at her, he was sitting straight upright on his chair and facing the happy crowd in the bar. How were those men able to be so casual? How did they think of things to say?

"How well do you know Frank and Lindy?" she asked.

"I work with Frank." He glanced over at her, then looked back at the happy, untroubled people in the bar. "We're in the same office."

"That's all? You don't see him after work?"

He shook his head.

"You made a big impression on Frank," she said. "He seems to think...Bob, would you mind looking at me, Bob? When I'm talking to you?"

Bunting cleared his throat and turned to face her. "Sorry."

"Is anything wrong? Anything I should know about? Do I look just like the person you hated most in the fourth grade?"

"No, I like the way you look," Bunting said.

"Frank acted like you were this real swinger. This wild man. 'Long fangs, Marty,' he says to me, 'this guy has got long, long fangs,' you know how Frank talks. This means he likes you. So I figured if Frank *Herko* liked you so much, how bad could you be? Because Frank Herko acts like a real asshole, but underneath, he's a sweetheart." She sipped her wine and continued looking at him coolly. "So I got all dolled up and took the train into Manhattan, figuring at least I might get some fun out of the evening, go to some clubs, maybe a good restaurant, meet this wild man, if I have to fight him off when it's all over, well, I can do that. But it's not like that, is it? You don't know any clubs—you don't really go out much, do you, Bobby?"

Bunting stood up and took a twenty out of his wallet. He was blushing so hard his ears felt twice their normal size. He put the money down on the table and said, "I'm sorry, I didn't mean to waste your time."

Marty grinned. "Hold on, will you?" She reached across the table and grabbed his wrist. "Don't act that way, I'm just saying you're different from what I expected. Sit down. Please. Don't be so…"

Bunting sat down, and she let go of his wrist. He could still feel her fingers around him. The sensation made him feel slightly dizzy. He was looking at her pale clever pretty face.

"So *scared*," she said. "There's no reason for that. Let's just sit here and talk. In a while, we can go out and eat somewhere. Or we could even eat here. Okay?"

"Sure," he said, recovering. "We can just sit here and talk."

"So say something," Marty said. She frowned. "Do you always sweat this much? Or is it just me?"

He wiped his forehead. "I, uh, had a kind of funny week. Things have been affecting me in an odd way. I broke up with somebody a little while ago."

"Frank told me. Me, too. That's why he thought we ought to meet each other. But I think you ought to think of another topic."

"I don't have any topics," Bunting said.

"Guys all talk about sports. I like sports. Honest, I really do. I'm a Yankee fan from way back. And I like Islanders games. But basketball is my favorite sport. Who do you like? Larry Bird, I bet—you look like a Larry Bird type. Guys who like Larry Bird never like Michael Jordan, I don't know why."

"Michael who?" Bunting said.

"Okay, football. Phil Simms. The Jets. The good old Giants. Lawrence Taylor."

"I hate football."

"Okay, what about music? What kind of music do you like? You ever hear house music?"

Bunting imagined a house like a child's drawing, two windows on either side of a simple door, dancing to notes spilling from the chimney attached to its pointed roof.

Marty tilted her head and smiled at him. "On second thought, I bet you like classical music. You sit around in your place and listen to symphonies and stuff like that. You make yourself a little martini and then you put on a little Beethoven, right? And then you're right in the groove. I like classical music sometimes, too, I think it's good."

"People are too interested in sports and music," Bunting said. "All they talk about is some game they saw on television, or some series, or some record. It's like there isn't anything else."

"You forgot one," she said. "You forgot money."

"That's right—they pay too much attention to money."

"So what should they pay attention to?"

"Well…" He looked up, for the moment wholly distracted from his embarrassment and discomfort. It seemed to him that there existed an exact answer to this question, and that he knew it. "Well, more important things." He raised his hands, as if he could catch the answer while it flew past him.

"More important than sports, television, and music. Not to mention money."

"Yes. None of that is important at all—it's worthless, when you come right down to it."

"So what is important?" She looked at him with her eyes narrowed behind her big glasses. "I'm dying to hear about it."

"Um, what's inside us."

"What's *inside* us? What does that mean?"

Bunting made another large vague gesture with his hands. "I sort of think God is inside us." This sentence came out of his mouth by itself, and it startled him as much as it did Marty. "Something like God is inside us. Outside of us, too." Then he found a way to say it. "God is what lets us see."

"So you're religious."

"No, the funny thing is, I'm not. I haven't gone to church in twenty-five years." He flattened his hands against his eyes for a moment, then took them away. His whole face had a naked look, as if he had just taken off a pair of eyeglasses. "Let's say you're just walking down the street. Let's say you're not thinking about anything in particular. You're trying to get to work, and you're even a little worried about something—the rent, or the way your boss was acting, or something. You're absolutely, completely, inside the normal world. And then something happens—a car backfires, or a woman with a gorgeous voice starts to sing behind you—and suddenly you see what's really there—that everything, absolutely everything is alive. The whole world is one living thing, and that living thing is just *beating* with life. Every rock, every blade of grass, every speck of dust, every raindrop, even the windshield wipers and the headlights, it's like you're floating in space, or no, it's like you're gone, disappeared, like you don't really exist anymore in the old way at all because you're the same as everything else, no more alive, no more conscious, *just* as alive, *just* as conscious, everything is overflowing, light streams and pours out of every little detail…" Bunting fought down the desire to cry.

"I'll give you one thing, it makes a double play against Los Angeles sound pretty small."

"The double play would be part of it, too," he said, understanding that too now. "Us sitting here is part of it. We're talking, and that's a big part of it. If churches were about what they're supposed to be about, they'd open their windows and concentrate on us sitting here. Look at that, they'd say, look at all that beauty and feeling, look at that radiance, that incredible radiance, that's what's holy. But do you know what they say instead?" He hitched his chair closer to her, and took another big gulp of his drink. "Maybe they really know all this, I think some of them must know it, it must be their secret, but instead, what they say is just the *opposite*. The world is evil and ugly, they say—turn your back on it. You need blood, they say—you need sacrifice. We're back to savages jumping around in front of a fire. Kill that child, kill that goat, the body is sinful and the world is bad. Ignore it long enough and you'll get a reward in heaven. People get old believing in this, they get sick and forgetful, they begin to fade out of the world without ever having seen it."

Marty was looking at him intently, and her mouth was open. She blinked when he stopped talking. "I can see why Frank is impressed with you. He can go on like this for hours. You must have a great time at work."

"We never talk about this at work. I never talked about it with anybody until now." It came to Bunting that he was sitting at a table with a pretty woman. He was in the world and enjoying himself. He was on a date, talking. It was not a problem. He was like the men in the bar behind him, talking to their dates. He wondered if he could tell Marty about the baby bottles.

"Didn't you talk like this with your old girl-friend?"

Bunting shook his head. "She was only interested in her career. She would have thought I was crazy."

"Well, I think you're crazy, too," Marty said. "But that's okay. Frank is crazy in another way, and among other, less harmless things, my old boyfriend was crazy about doo-wop music. Johnny Maestro? He worshipped Johnny Maestro. He thought it summed it all up."

"I suppose it did," Bunting said. "But no more than anything else."

"Did you get a lot of this stuff out of books? Do you read a lot?"

Another flare went off in Bunting's brain, and he took another gulp of his drink, waving his free hand in the air, semaphoring that she hadn't quite understood matters, but that he had plenty to say about her question. "Books!" he said after he had swallowed. "You wouldn't believe what I've..." He shook his head. She was smiling at him. "Think about what reading a book is really *like*. A novel, I mean—you're reading a novel. What's happening? You're in another world, right? Somebody made it, somebody selected everything in it, and so suddenly you're not in your apartment anymore, you're walking along this mountain road, or you're sitting on top of a horse. You look out and you see things. What you see is partly what the guy put there for you to see, and partly what you make up on the basis of that. Everything means something, because it was all chosen. Everything you see, touch, feel, smell, everything you notice and everything you think, is organized to take you somewhere. Do you see? Everything *glows!* In paintings, too, don't you suppose? There's some force pushing away at all the details, making them *bulge*, making them *sing*. Because the act of painting or writing about a leaf or a house or whatever, if the guy does it right, amounts to saying: I saw the amazing overflowing life in this thing, and now you can see it, too. So wake up!" He gestured with both arms, like a conductor calling for a great swell of sound.

"Have you ever thought about becoming a teacher?" Marty asked. "You get all fired up, Bobby, you'd be great in a classroom."

"I just want to say something." Bunting held his hands over his heart. "This is the greatest night of my life. I never really felt like this before. At least, not since I was really small, three or four, or something. I feel wonderful!"

"Well, you're certainly not nervous anymore," Marty said. "But I still say you're religious."

"I never heard of any religion that preaches about this, did you? If you hear of one, let me know and I'll sign up. It has to be a church that says, Don't come in here, stay outside in the weather. Wake up and open your eyes. What we do in here, with the crosses and stuff, that's just to remind you of what's *really* sacred."

"You're something else," she said, laughing. "You and Frank Herko are quite the pair. The two of you must get that office all stirred up."

"Maybe we should." For a giddy instant, Bunting saw himself and shaggy, overbearing Frank Herko conducting loud debates over the partition. He would speak as he was speaking now, and Frank would respond with delight and abandon, and the two of them would carry on their talks after work, in apartments and restaurants and bars. It was a vision of a normal and joyous life—he would call up Frank Herko at his apartment, and Frank would say, Why don't you come on over? Bring Marty, we'll go out for dinner, have a little fun. Bunting and Marty were smiling at each other.

"You're sort of like Frank, you know. You like saying outrageous things. You're not at all the way I thought you were when I came in. I mean, I liked you, and I thought you were interesting, but I thought it might be kind of a long evening. You don't mind my saying that now? I really don't want to hurt your feelings, and I shouldn't be, because you seem so different now. I mean, I never heard anybody talk that way before, not even Frank. It might be crazy, but it's fascinating."

Nobody had ever told Bunting he was fascinating before this, especially not a young woman staring at him with wonderful blue eyes past a fall of pure black hair. He realized, and this was one of the most triumphant moments of his life, that he could very likely bring this amazing young woman back to his apartment.

Then he remembered what his apartment—his room—actually looked like, and what he had done to it.

"Don't start blushing again," Marty said. "It's just a compliment. You're an interesting man, and you hardly know it." She reached across the table and rested her fingers lightly on the back of his hand. "Why don't we finish these drinks and order some food? It's Friday. We don't have to go anywhere else. This is fine. I'm enjoying myself."

Marty's light cool fingers felt as heavy as anvils on his skin. A wave of pure guilt made him pull his hand away. She was still smiling at him, but a shadow passed behind her wonderful eyes. "I have to do something," he said. "I shouldn't have let myself forget," he said. "There must be a telephone in this place somewhere." He began looking wildly around the restaurant.

"You have to call someone?"

"It's urgent, I'm sorry, I can't believe I've been acting like..." Bunting wiped his face and pushed himself away from the table and stood up. He moved clumsily toward the people standing at the bar.

"Like *what?*" she asked, but he was already pushing clumsily through the crowd.

Bunting found a pay telephone outside the men's room. He scooped change out of his pockets and stacked it up. Then he dialled the area code for Battle Creek and his parents' number. He dropped in most of the money. The phone rang and rang, and Bunting fidgeted and cupped his ear against the roar of voices from the bar. Finally his mother answered.

"Mom! How are you? How'd it go?"

"Yes, who is this?"

"Bobby. It's Bobby."

"Bobby isn't here," she said.

"No, *I'm* Bobby, Mom. How are you feeling?"

"Fine. Why wouldn't I feel fine?"

"Did you see the doctor today?"

"Why would I see him?" She sounded sharp, almost angry. "That was stupid. I don't have to see *him*, listen to your father gripe about the money for the rest of his life."

"Didn't you have an appointment?"

"Did I?"

"I think so," he said, feeling his grip on reality loosen.

"Well, what if I did? This isn't Russia. Your father wanted to bully me about the money, that's all it is. I pretended—just sat in my car, that's all I did. He wants to humiliate me, that's what it is, thirty-seven years of humiliation."

"He didn't go with you?"

"He *couldn't*, there wasn't any *appointment*. And when I came home, I drove and drove, I kept seeing Kellog's and the sanitarium, but I never knew where I was and so I had to keep driving, and then, like a miracle, I saw I was turning into our street, and I was so mad at him I swore I'd never ever go to that doctor again."

"You got lost driving home?" His body felt hot all over.

"Now, you stop talking about that. You sound like *him*. I want to know about that beautiful girlfriend of yours. Tell me about Veronica. Someday you have to bring that girl home, Bobby. We want to meet her."

"I'm not going out with her anymore," Bunting said. "I wrote you."

"You're just like that horrible old crosspatch. Brutal is the word for him. Brutal all his life, brutal brutal brutal. Says things just to *confuse* me, and then he gets upset when I want to do a little wash, acts as if I haven't been his punching bag for the past thirty years—"

Bunting heard only heavy breathing for a moment. "Mom?"

"I don't know who you are, and I wish you'd stop calling," she said. Bunting heard his father's voice, loud and indistinct, and his mother said, "Oh, you can leave me alone, too." Then he heard a startled outcry.

"Hello, what's going on?" Bunting said. All the sounds from Battle Creek had dwindled into a muffled silence overwhelmed by the din from the bar. His father had put his hand over the mouthpiece. This almost certainly meant that he was yelling. "Someone talk to me!" Bunting shouted, and the yelling in the bar abruptly ceased. Bunting hunched his shoulders and tried to burrow into the hood over the telephone.

"All right, who is this?" his father asked.

"Bob, it's Bobby," he said.

"You've got some nerve, calling up out of the blue, but you never did care much about what anybody else might be going through, did you? Look, I know you're sensitive and all that, but this isn't the best time to give us bullshit about your little girlfriends. You got your mother all upset, and she was upset enough already, believe me." He hung up.

Bunting replaced the receiver. He was not at all clear about what was going on in Battle Creek. It had seemed that his mother had forgotten who he was during the course of their worrying conversation. He pushed his way through the men and women at the bar and came out into the restaurant where a young woman with a round face framed in black hair was looking at him curiously from one of the rear tables. It took him a moment to remember her name. He tried to smile at her, but his face would not work right.

"What happened to you?" she asked.

"This isn't...um, I can't, ah...I'm afraid that I have to go home."

Her face hardened with a recognition: in an instant, all the sympathy dropped away. "We were having a nice time, and you go make a phone call, and now everything's off?"

Bunting shrugged and looked at his feet. "It's a personal thing—I can't really explain it—but, uh—"

"*But, uh*, that's it? What happened to, 'This is the greatest night of my life'?" She squinted at him. "Oh, boy. I guess I get it. You ran out, didn't you? You thought you could get through an evening, and then you realized you can't, so you called your guy. And everything you said wasn't really you, it was just— just that crap you take. You're pathetic."

"I don't know what you're talking about," Bunting said. His misery seemed to be compounding itself second by second.

"I know guys like you," she said, her eyes blazing at him. "One in particular." She held out an imperious hand for the checkroom ticket. "I know a few inadequate children who can't handle relationships, one in particular, but I thought I was all done hanging around a guy who spent half the night making phone calls and the other half in the bathroom—and I guess I really am done! Because I'm going!" She retrieved her coat and shoved her arms into its sleeves. People at the other tables were staring at them.

"You must have the wrong idea about something," Bunting said.

"Oh, that's good," she said. She buttoned her coat. Her small face seemed cold, a cold white stone with a red smear near the bottom. "Sleep on it, if you do sleep, see if you can come up with something a little snappier." Marty walked quickly through the tables, passed the lounging headwaiter, and went outside. Frigid air swept into the restaurant as the door closed on the empty darkness.

Bunting paid for the drinks and noticed that the waitress would not look directly at him. An artificial quiet had settled on the bar. Bunting put on his coat and wandered outside, feeling lost and aimless. He had no appetite. He buttoned up his coat and watched cars stream toward him down the wide avenue. A short distance to his left, the avenue ended at a massive arch which stood at the entrance to a park. He had no idea where he was. That didn't matter: all places were the same place. Traffic continued to come toward him out of the dark, and he realized that he was in Battle Creek, Michigan—he was back in Battle Creek, downtown in the business district, a long way from home.

X

WHEN JESUS FLEW TO HEAVEN HE HAD
wounds in his hands and feet, they had torn his flesh
and killed him on a cross, there was blood on the
ground, and when he rolled the rock away in his
dusty robe he left bloody palm prints on the rock.

Jesus said, So you have some fucking doubts,
Bobby? Take a look at this. And opened his clothes
and showed Bunting the great open wound in his
side. Go on, he said, stick your goddamned hand
in it, stick your mitt in there, how about them goddamn apples, Bobby? You get it, you get it now, good
buddy? This shit is for real.

And Jesus walked on his bleeding feet through
Battle Creek, leaving his bloodstains on sidewalks
unseen by the assholes who had never been wounded
by anything more serious than a third martini, and
who had never wounded anyone else with a weapon
deadlier than an insult. There was a savage grin on
his face. He slammed the palm of a hand against the
side of one of those little houses, and blood squirted
onto the peeling paint. Holy holy holy. The palm
print was holy, the flecks of paint were holy, the cries
of pain and sorrow, too.

Go home, you little asshole, said Jesus. You're
never gonna get it, never. But neither do most peo-

ple, so that part's okay. Go home and read a book. That'll do—it's a piss-poor way to get there, but I guess it's about the best you can do.

Suffer the little children, said Jesus, suffer everybody else, too. You think this shit is easy?

Still muttering to himself, Jesus turned off on a side street, his bloody footprints following after him, his thin robe whipping around him in the wind, and Bunting saw the frame houses of working-class Battle Creek all around him. Some were covered with hideous brick-face, some with grainy tar paper that peeled away from the seams around the window frames. Most of these houses had porches where skeletal furniture turned brittle in the cold, and birdbaths and shrines to Mary stood in a few tiny front yards. Before one of these unhappy two-story frame houses his parents had posed for the only photograph ever taken of the two of them together, a testament to ignorance, incompatibility, resentment, violence, and disorder. His father scowls out from under the brim of his hat, his mother twitches. Holy holy holy. From this chaos, from this riot, the overpowering sacred bounty. He was standing on his old street, Bunting realized, the ultimate sample in this dwindled and partial world of blazing real life. Jesus' bloody palm print shone from the ugly wall, even uglier now in winter when the dirty chipping paint looked like a skin disease. Here was his childhood, which he had not been intended to escape—

its smallness and meanness had been supposed to accompany him always.

Bunting stared at the shabby building in which his childhood had happened, and heard the old screams, the grunts and shrieks of pain and passion, sail through the thin walls. This was the bedrock. His childhood reached forth and touched him with a cold, cold finger. He could not survive it now, he could not even bear to witness a tenth of it. But neither could he live without it.

He turned around and found that he had left Battle Creek and walked all the way from Washington Square to the Upper West Side. Across the street, on the other side of several hundred jostling, honking cars, stood his apartment building. Home again.

XI

BUNTING'S WEEKEND WAS GLACIAL. HE had trouble getting out of bed, and remembered to eat only when he realized that the sun had gone down. He felt so tired it was difficult to walk to the bathroom, and fell asleep in front of the television, watching programs that seemed without point or plot. It was all one great formless story, a story with no internal connections, and its incoherence made it watchable.

On Sunday afternoon Bunting scratched his face and remembered that he had not bathed or shaved since Friday evening. He took off the clothes he'd worn since Saturday morning, showered, shaved, dressed in grey slacks and a sport jacket, put on his coat, and went around the corner through brittle wintry air to the diner. The man at the register and the counterman treated him normally. He ordered something from the enormous menu, ate what he ordered without tasting it, and forgot it as soon as he was done. When he walked back out into the cold he realized that he could buy more baby bottles. He had to finish the wall he had begun, and there was another wall he could cover with bottles, if he chose—he was under no real compulsion to do this, he knew, but it would be like finishing an old project. Bunting had always liked to complete his projects. There were several other things he could do with baby bottles, too, once he got started.

He walked to the cash machine and took out three hundred dollars, leaving only five hundred and change in his account. At the drugstore he bought a gross of mixed bottles and another gross of mixed nipples, and asked for them to be delivered. Then he walked again out into the cold and turned toward his building. His entire attitude toward the bottles, even the redecoration project, had changed—he could remember his first, passionate purchases, the haste and embarrassment, the sheer weight of the need. Bunting supposed that this calm, passive state was a dull version of what most people felt all the time. It was probably what they called sanity. Sanity was what took over when you got too tired for anything else. He stopped off at the liquor store and bought two litres of vodka and a bottle of cognac.

This time when he walked out into the cold, it came to him that Veronica had never existed. Of course he had always known at some level that his executive, Swiss-born mistress was a fantasy, but it seemed to him that he had never quite admitted this to himself. He had lived with his stories for so long he had forgotten that they had begun as an excuse for not going back to Battle Creek.

Battle Creek had come to him instead, two nights ago. *Suffer the little children, suffer everybody, suffer suffer.* The furious, complaining Jesus had shown what was real. This dry, reduced world was what was left when He stormed back into His cave to lie down dead again. Bunting walked past the leavings of BANGO SKANK and JEEPY and let himself back into his room. He switched on the television and poured cold vodka into an Ama. Words and phrases of unbelievable ugliness, language murdered by carelessness and indifference, dead bleeding language, came from the television. People all over the nation listened to stuff like this every day and heard nothing wrong in it. Bunting watched the action on the screen for a moment, trying to make at least some kind of primitive sense out of it. A blonde man ran down a flight of stairs and punched another man in the face. The second man, taller and stronger than the first, collapsed and fell all the way down the stairs. A car sped down a highway, and lights flashed. Bunting sighed and snapped off the television.

Bunting wandered through the stacks of magazines and newspapers and picked up *The Lady in the Lake*. He wondered if the buzzing of the delivery boy would pull him out of the book and then remembered with a deepening sense of gloom—with something very close to despair—that he probably would not have to be pulled out of the book. He was sane now. Or, if that was an error of terminology, he was in the same relationship to the world that he had been in before everything had changed.

Bunting held his breath and opened the book. He let his eyes drop to the lines of print, which resolutely stayed on the page. He sighed again and sat down on the bed to read until the new baby bottles arrived.

It was another book—the details were the same but all the essentials had changed. Chris Lavery was apparently still alive, and Muriel Chess had been found in Little Fawn Lake, not in the bathroom of a mountain cabin. Crystal Kingsley was Derace Kingsley's wife, not his mother. All the particulars of weather, appearances, and speech, the entire atmosphere of the book, came to Bunting in a flawed and ordinary way, sentence by sentence. For Bunting, this way of reading was like having lost the ability, briefly and mysteriously gained, of being able to fly. He stumbled along after the sentences, remembering what had been. When the buzzer rang he put the book down with relief, and spent the rest of the night gluing bottles to his walls.

On Monday morning, Frank Herko came into his cubicle even before going into his own. His eyes looked twice their normal size, and his forehead was still red from the cold. Static electricity had given his hair a lively, unbridled, but stiff look, as if it had been starched or deep-fried. "What the hell went on?" he yelled as soon as he came in. Bunting could feel the attention of everyone else in the Data Entry room focusing on his cubicle.

"I don't know what you mean," he said.

Herko actually bared his teeth at him. His eyes grew even larger. He unzipped his down jacket, ripped it off his body, and startled Bunting by throwing it to the floor. "Then I'll try to tell you," he said, speaking so softly he was nearly whispering. "My girlfriend Lindy has a girlfriend. A person named Marty. This is a person she likes. Particularly likes. You could even go so far as to say that Marty is a person very dear to my friend Lindy, and that what affects Marty affects my girlfriend Lindy. So the little ups and downs of this person Marty's life, who by the way is also kind of dear to me, though not of course to the extent that she is dear to my friend, these ups and downs affect my friend Lindy and therefore, in a roundabout sort of way, also affect me." Frank leaned forward from the waist and extended his arms. "SO! When Marty has a bad experience with a guy she calls a sleazeball and blames this experience on her friend Lindy Berman and Lindy Berman's friend Frank HERKO, then Frank HERKO winds up eating SHIT! Is it starting to fall into place, Bobby? Are you starting to get why I asked you what the HELL happened?" He planted his fists on his hips and glowered, then shook his head and made a gesture with one arm that implored the universe to witness his frustration.

"It just didn't work out," Bunting said.

"Oh, is that right? You don't suppose you could go into a little more detail on that, could you?"

Bunting tried to remember why his date had ended. "My mother didn't make her doctor's appointment."

Herko stared at him pop-eyed. "Your mother… Does that make sense to you? You're out with a girl, you're supposed to be having a good time, you say,

Gee, Mom didn't get over to the doctor's, I guess I better SPLIT?"

"I'm sorry," Bunting said. "I'm not in a very good mood right now. I don't like it when you yell at me. That makes me feel very uneasy. I wish you'd leave me alone."

"Boy, you got it," Herko said. "You have got it, Bobby, in spades. But there are a few vital bits of information it has become extremely necessary for you to have in your possession, Bobby, and I am going to give them to you."

He stepped backward and saw his down jacket on the floor. He raised his eyes as if the jacket had disobediently conjured itself off a hook and thrown itself on the carpet. He leaned over and picked it up, ostentatiously folded it in half, and draped it over one arm. All this reminded Bunting sharply, even sickeningly, of his father. The affectation of delicacy had been a crucial part of his father's arsenal of scorn. Herko had probably reminded him of his father from the beginning; he had just never noticed it.

"One," Frank said. "I assumed you were going to act like a man. Funny, huh? I thought you would know that a man remembers his friends, and a man is grateful to his friends. A man does not act like a goddamn loony and bring down trouble on his friends. Two. A man does not run out on a woman. A man does not leave a woman in the middle of a restaurant—he acts like a MAN, damn it, and conducts himself like he knows what he's doing. Three.

She thought you were a drug addict, did that get through to you?"

"I didn't leave her alone, she left me alone," Bunting said.

"She thought you were a junkie!" Herko was yelling again. "She thought I fixed her up with a fucking cocaine freak, right after she broke up with a guy who put a restaurant, a house, and a car up his nose! That's…" Herko raised his arms and lifted his head, trying to find the right word. "That's…MISERABLE! DISGUSTING!"

Bunting stood up and grabbed his coat. His heart wanted to explode. It was not possible to spend another second in his cubicle. Frank Herko had become ten feet tall, and every one of his breaths drained all the air from Bunting's own lungs. His screams bruised Bunting's ears. Bunting was buttoning his coat before he realized that he was walking out of the cubicle and going home.

"Where the hell do you think you're going?" Herko yelled. "You can't leave!"

Unable to speak, nearly unable to see through the red mist that surrounded him, Bunting hurried out of the Data Entry room and fled down the corridor toward the elevator.

As soon as he got out of the building he felt a little better, but the woman who stood next to him on the uptown bus edged visibly away.

He could still hear Frank's huge, punishing voice. The world belonged to people like his father and Frank Herko, and people like himself lived in its potholes and corners.

Bunting got out of the bus and realized that he was talking to himself only when he saw himself in a shop window. He blushed, and would have apologized, but no one around him met his eye. He walked into the lobby of his apartment building and realized that it was not going to be possible for him to go back to work. He could never face Herko again, nor the other people who had overheard Frank's terrible yelling. That was finished. It was all over, like the fantasy of Veronica.

He got into the elevator, thinking that he seemed to be different from what he had thought he was, though it was hard to tell if this was for the better or the worse. In the old days, he would have been figuring out where to go to get another job, and now all he wanted to do was to get back into his room, pour himself a drink, and open a book. Of course all of these had also changed, room, drink, and book.

By the time he pushed his key into the lock he realized that he was no longer so frightened. In the psychic background, the waves of Frank Herko's voice crashed and rumbled on a distant beach. Bunting decided to give himself something like a week to recover from the events of the past few days, then to go out and look for another job. A week was a comfortable time. Monday to Monday. He hung up his coat and poured a drink into a clean Ama. Then he collapsed onto his bed and let his head fall back on the pillow. He groaned with satisfaction.

For a time he merely sucked at his bottle and let his body sink into his wrinkled sheets. In a week, he told himself, he would get out of bed. He'd shave and dress in clean clothes and go outside and nail down a new job. He'd sit in front of another computer terminal and type in a lifetime's worth of mumbo jumbo. Soon there would be another Veronica or Carol, an Englishwoman or a Texan or a Cuban with an MBA from Wharton who was just finding her sea legs at Citibank. It would be the same thing all over again, and it would be terrible, but it would be okay. Sometimes it would even be sort of nice.

He sucked air, and lifted the bottle in surprise and found that it was empty. It seemed that he had just declared a private holiday. Bunting rolled off the bed and went through the litter to the refrigerator. He dumped more vodka into the bottle. Vodka could get you through these little blue periods.

Bunting closed the freezer door, screwed the top onto the bottle, and held the nipple clenched between his teeth while he surveyed his room. One week, then back into the world. Bunting remembered his vision of the raging Jesus who had stormed through working-class Battle Creek. Suffer the little children.

He crossed to his bed and picked up the telephone. "Okay," he said, sucked from the bottle, and sat down. "Why not?

"I ought to," he said.

He dialed the area code for Battle Creek, then the first three digits of his parents' number.

"Just thought I'd call," he said. He pulled more vodka into his mouth.

"How are things? I don't want to upset anybody."

He dialled the last four numbers and listened to the phone ring in that little house so far away. Finally his father answered, not with "Hello," but with "Yeah."

"Hi, Dad, this is Bobby," he said. "Just thought I'd call. How are things?"

"Fine, why wouldn't they be?" his father said.

"Well, I didn't want to upset anybody."

"Why would we get upset? You know how your mother and I feel. We enjoy your calls."

"You do?"

"Well, sure. Don't get enough of 'em." There was a small moment of silence, "Got anything special on your mind, Bobby?"

It was as if the other night had never happened. This was how it went, Bunting remembered. If you forgot about something, it went away.

"I guess I was wondering about Mom," he said. "She sounded a little confused, the other night."

"Guess she was," his father said in an abrupt, dismissive voice. "She gets that way, now and then. *I* can't do anything about it, Bobby. How're things at work? Okay?"

"Things could be better," Bunting said, and immediately regretted it.

"Oh?" Now his father's voice was hard and biting. "What happened, you get fired? They fired you, didn't they? You screwed up and they fired you."

He could hear his father breathing hard, stoking himself up like a steam engine.

For a second it seemed that his father was right: he had screwed up, and they had fired him. "No," he said. "They didn't. I'm not fired."

"But you're not at work, either. It's nine o'clock in the morning here, so it's ten where you are, and Bobby Bunting is still in his apartment. So you lost your job. I knew it was gonna happen."

"No, it didn't," Bunting said. "I just left early."

"Sure. You left at eight-thirty on Monday morning. What do you call that, premature retirement? I call it getting fired. Just don't try to kid me about it, Bobby, I know what kind of person you are." He inhaled. "And don't expect any money from the old folks, okay? Remember all those meals at fancy restaurants and all those trips to Europe, and you'll know where your money went. If you ever had any, and if any of that stuff was true, which is something I have my doubts about."

"I took the day off," Bunting said. "Maybe I'll take off tomorrow, too. I'm taking care of a few details around here."

"Yeah, those kind of details are likely to take care of you, if you don't watch out."

"Look," said Bunting, stung. "I'm not fired. You hear me? Nobody fired me. I took the day off, because somebody got on my back. I don't know why you never believe me about anything."

"Do you want me to remind you about your whole life, back here? I know who you are, Bobby, let's leave it at that." His father inhaled again, so loudly it sounded as if he had put the telephone into his mouth. He was calming himself. "Don't get me wrong, you got your good points, same as everybody else. Maybe you just ought to cut down on the wild social life, and stop trying to make up for never going out when you were a teenager, that's all. There's responsibilities. Responsibilities were never your strong point. But maybe you changed. Fine. Okay?"

Bunting felt as if he had been mugged on a dark street. It was like having Frank Herko yell at him about manhood all over again.

"Let me ask you something," he said, and pulled another mouthful of Popov out of the Ama. "Have you ever thought that you saw what reality really was?"

"Jesus wept."

"Wait. I mean something by that. Didn't you ever have a time when you saw that everything was alive?"

"Stop right there, Bobby, I don't want to hear this shit all over again. Just shut your trap, if you know what's good for you."

"What do you mean?" Bunting was almost yelling. "You mean I can't talk about it? Why can't I talk about it?"

"Because it's crazy, you dummy," his father said. "I want you to hear this, Bobby. You're nothing special. You got that? You worried your mother enough already, so keep your trap shut. For your own good."

Bunting felt astonishingly small. His father's voice had pounded him down into childhood, and he was now about three feet tall. "I can't talk anymore."

"Sleep it off and straighten up," his father said. "I mean it."

Bunting let the phone slide back into the cradle and grabbed for the Ama.

By the time he decided to get out of bed, he was so drunk that he had trouble navigating across the room and into the bathroom. As he peed, a phrase of his father's came back to him, and his urine splattered off the wall. *I don't want to hear this shit all over again.* All over again? If he weren't drunk, he thought, he would understand some fact he did not presently understand. But because he was drunk, he couldn't. Neither could he go outside. Bunting reeled back to his bed and passed out.

He woke up in the darkness with a headache and a vast, encompassing feeling of shame and sorrow. His life was nothing—it had always been nothing, it would always be nothing. There could be no release. The things he had seen, his experiences of ecstasy, the moment he had tried to describe to Marty, all were illusion. In a week he would go back to Data-ComCorp, and everything would return to normal. Probably they would just take him back—he wasn't important enough to fire. The only difference would be that Frank Herko would ignore him.

His whole problem was that he always forgot he was nothing special.

He promised himself that he would stop making things up. There would be no more imaginary love affairs. Bunting walked over to his window and looked down upon men and women in winter coats and hats who had normal, unglamorous, realistic lives. They looked cold. He got back into bed as if into a coffin.

XII

THE NEXT MORNING, BUNTING POURED all of his vodka and cognac down the sink. Then he washed the dishes that had accumulated since his last washing. He looked at the sacks of garbage stowed away here and there, put the worst of them into large plastic bags, and took them all downstairs to the street. Back in his apartment, he swept and scrubbed for several hours. He changed his sheets and organized the magazines and newspapers into neat piles. Then he washed the bathroom floor and soaked in the tub for half an hour. He dried himself, brushed his teeth, combed his hair, and went straight back to bed. One of these days, he told himself, he would begin regular exercise.

The next day, he fought down the impulse to get another bottle of vodka and went to the supermarket on Broadway and bought a bag of carrots, a bag of celery, cartons of fruit juice and low-fat milk, a loaf of whole-grain bread, and a container of cholesterol-free margarine. Such a diet would keep the raging Jesus at bay.

Bunting spent most of Thursday lying down. He ate two carrots, three celery sticks, and one slice of dry bread. The bread tasted particularly good. He drank all of his fruit juice. In the evening, he tried switching on the television, but what came out was a stream of language so ugly it squeaked with pain. He fell soundly asleep at nine-thirty, was awakened by the sound of gunshots around three in the morning, and went promptly back to sleep.

On Friday he rose, showered, dressed in a conservative grey suit, ate a carrot and drank two or three ounces of papaya juice, put on his coat, and went outside for the first time since Monday morning. It was a bright brisk day, and the air, though not as fresh as that of the Montana plains in 1878 or Los Angeles in 1944, seemed startlingly clean and pure. Even on Upper Broadway, Bunting thought he could smell the sea. The outline of a body had been chalked on a roped-off portion of the sidewalk, and as Bunting walked between two parked cars and stepped down onto unsanitary, untidy Broadway to walk alongside the traffic in dazzling sunlight, he merely glanced at the white outline of the body and then firmly looked away and continued moving toward the traffic light and the open sidewalk.

Bunting walked for miles. He looked at the watches in Tourneau's windows, at the shoes in Church Brothers, the pocket calculators and compact disc players in a string of windows on lower Fifth Avenue. He came at length to Battery Park, and sat for a moment, looking out toward the Statue of Liberty. He was in the world, surrounded by people and things; the breeze that touched him touched everyone else, too. To Bunting, this world seemed new and almost undamaged, barren in a fashion only he had once known and now wished nearly to forget.

If a tree fell in the forest, it would not make a sound, no, none.

He began walking back uptown, remembering how he had once sat comfortably astride a horse named Shorty and how a worried perfume executive in a flannel suit had handed him a photograph of his mother. These experiences too could be sealed within a leaden casket and pushed overboard into the great psychic sea. They were aberrations: silent and weightless exceptions to a general rule. He would get old in his little room, drinking iced tea and papaya juice out of baby bottles. He would outlive his parents. Both of them. Everybody did that.

He took a bus up Broadway, and got off several blocks before his building because he wanted to walk a little more. On the corner a red-faced man in a shabby plaid coat sat on a camp chair behind a display of used paperback books. Bunting paused to look over the titles for a Luke Short or a Max Brand, but saw mainly romance novels with titles like *Love's Savage Bondage* or *Sweet Merciless Kiss*. These titles, and the disturbing covers that came with them, threatened to remind Bunting of Marty seated across from him in a Greenwich Village restaurant, and he stepped back from the array to banish even the trace of this memory. A cover unlike the others met his eye, and he took in the title, *Anna Karenina*, and realized that he had heard of the book somewhere—of course he had never read it, it was nothing like the sort of books he usually read, but he was sure that it was supposed to be very good. He bent down and picked up and opened it at random. He leaned toward the page in the light of the street lamp and read. *Before the early dawn all was hushed. Nothing was to be heard but the night sounds of the frogs that never ceased in the marsh, and the horses snorting in the mist that rose over the meadow before the morning.*

A thrill went through his body, and he turned the page and read another couple of sentences. *A slight wind rose, and the sky looked grey and sullen. The gloomy moment that usually precedes the dawn had come, the full triumph of light over darkness.*

Bunting felt a strange desire to weep: he wanted to stand there for a long time, leafing through this miraculous book.

A voice said, "World's greatest realistic novel, hands down." Bunting looked up to meet the uncommonly intelligent gaze of the pudgy red-faced man in the camp chair.

"That right?"

"Anybody says different, he's outta his fuckin' mind." He wiped his nose on his sleeve. "One dollar."

Bunting fished a dollar from his pocket and leaned over the rows of bright covers to give it to the man. "What makes it so great?" he asked.

"Understanding. *Depth* of understanding. Unbelievable responsiveness to detail linked to amazing clarity of vision."

"Yeah," Bunting said, "yeah, that's it." He clutched the book to his chest and turned away toward his apartment building.

He placed the book on his chair and sat on the bed and looked at its cover. In a few sentences, *Anna Karenina* had brought shining bits of the world to him—it was as close as you could get to *The Buffalo Hunter* experience and still be sane. Everything was so close that it was almost like being inside it. The two short passages he had read had brought the other world within him, which had once seemed connected to a great secret truth about the world as a whole, once again into being—had awakened it by touching it. Bunting was almost afraid of this power. He had to have the book, but he was not sure that he could read it.

Bunting jumped up off the bed and ate two slices of whole-grain bread and a couple of carrots. Then he put his coat on and went back to the cash machine at the bank and to the drugstore across the street.

That night he lay in bed, enjoying the slight ache in his legs all the walking had given him and drinking warm milk from his old Prentiss. Beneath him, odd and uncomfortable but perfect all the same, was the construction he had made from eighty round plastic Evenflos and a tube of epoxy, a lumpy blanket of baby bottles that nestled into and warmed itself against his body. He had thought of making a sheet of baby bottles a long time ago, when he had been thinking about fakirs and beds of nails, and finally making the sheet now was a whimsical reference to that time when he had thought mainly about baby bottles. Bunting thought that sometime he could take off all the nipples and fill every one of the Evenflos beneath him with warm milk. It would be like going to bed with eighty little hot water bottles.

He held the slightly battered copy of *Anna Karenina* up before him and looked at the cover illustration of a train which had paused at a country station to take on fuel or food for its passengers. A snowstorm swirled around the front of the locomotive. The illustration seemed filled with the same luminous, almost alarming reality as the sentences he had found at random within the book, and Bunting knew that this sense of promise and immediacy came from the memory of those passages. Opening the book at all seemed to invoke a great risk, but if Bunting could have opened it to those sentences in which the horses snorted in the mist and the wind sprang up under a grey morning sky, he would have done so instantly. His eyes drooped, and the little train in the illustration threw upward a white flag of steam and jolted forward through the falling snow.

XIII

MONDAY MORNING THE TELEPHONE rang with a fussy, importunate clamour that all but announced the presence of Frank Herko on the other end of the line—Bunting, who was in the fourth day of his sobriety, could imagine Herko grimacing and cursing as the phone went unanswered. Bunting continued chewing on a slice of dry bread, and looked at his watch. It was ten o'clock. Herko had finally admitted that he was not coming in again, and was trying to bully him back to DataComCorp. Bunting had no intention of answering the telephone. Frank Herko and the job in the Data Entry room dwindled as they shrank into the past. He swallowed the last of his papaya juice and reminded himself to pick up more fruit juices that morning. At last, on the thirteenth ring, the telephone fell silent.

Bunting thought of the horses snorting in the cold morning mist when everything else was silent but the frogs, and a shiver went through him.

He stood up from the table and looked around his room. It was pretty radical. He thought it might look a little better if he got rid of all the newspapers and magazines—his room could never look ordinary anymore, but what he had done would mean more if the whole room was a little cleaner. The nipples of baby bottles jutted out from two walls, and a blanket of baby bottles, like a sheet of chain mail, covered his bed. If there were very little else in the room, Bunting saw, it would be as purposeful as a museum exhibit. He could get rid of the television. All he needed was one table, one chair, two lamps, and his bed. His room would be stark as a monument. And the monument would be to everything that was missing. Bunting was a little uncertain as to what precisely was missing, but he didn't think it could be summed up easily.

He washed his plate and glass and put them on the drying rack. Then he unplugged his television set, picked it up, unlocked his door, and carried the set out into the hall. He took it down past the elevators and set it on the floor. Then he turned around and hurried back into his apartment.

Bunting spent the morning stuffing the magazines and newspapers into black garbage bags and taking them downstairs to the sidewalk. On his fourth or fifth trip, he noticed that the television had disappeared from the hallway. BANGO SKANK or JEEPY had a new toy. Gradually, Bunting's room lost its old enclosed look. There were the two walls covered with jutting bottles, the wall with the windows that overlooked the brownstones, and the kitchen alcove. There was his bed and the bedside chair. In front of the kitchen alcove stood his little dining table. He had uncovered another chair which had been concealed under a mound of papers, and this too he took out into the hallway for his neighbors.

When he came up from taking out the last of the garbage bags, he closed and locked the door behind him, pulled the police bar into its slot, and inspected his territory. A bare wooden floor, with dusty squares where stacks of newspapers had stood, extended toward him from the exterior wall. Without the newspapers, the distance between himself and the windows seemed immense. For the first time, Bunting noticed the streaks on the glass. The bright daylight turned them silver and cast long rectangles on the floor. Rigid baby bottles stuck out of the wall on both sides, to his right going toward the bathroom door and the kitchen alcove, and to his left, extending toward his bed. The wall above and beyond the bed was also covered with a mat of jutting baby bottles. A wide blanket of baby bottles, half-covering a flat pillow and a white blanket, lay across his bed.

After a lunch of carrots, celery, and bread, Bunting poured hot water and soap into a bucket and washed his floor. Then he poured out the filthy water, started again, and washed the table and the kitchen counters. After that he scrubbed even his bathroom—sink, toilet, floor, and tub. Large brown mildew stains blotted the shower curtain, and Bunting carefully unhooked it from the plastic rings, folded it into quarters, and took it downstairs and stuffed it into a garbage can.

He went to bed hungry but not painfully so, his back and shoulders tingling from the work, and his legs still aching from his long walk down the length of Manhattan. He lay atop the blanket of bottles, and pulled the sheet and woollen blanket over his body. He picked up the old paperback copy of *Anna Karenina* and opened it with trembling hands. For a second it seemed that the sentences were going to lift up off the page and claim him, and his heart tightened with both fear and some other, more anticipatory emotion. But his gaze met the page, and he stayed within his body and his room, and read. *And all at once she thought of the man crushed by the train the day she had first met Vronsky, and she knew what she had to do. With a light, rapid step she went down the steps that led from the water tank to the rails and stopped close to the approaching train.*

Bunting shuddered and fell into exhausted sleep.

He was walking through a landscape of vacant lots and cement walls in a city street that might have been New York or Battle Creek. Broken bottles and pages from old newspapers lay in the street. Here and there across the weedy lots, tenements rose into the grey air. His legs ached, and his feet hurt, and it was difficult for him to follow the man walking along ahead of him, whose pale robe filled and billowed in the cold wind. The man was slightly taller than Bunting, and his dark hair blew about his head. Untroubled by the winter wind, the man strode along, increasing the distance between himself and Bunting with every step. Bunting did not know why he had to follow this strange man, but that was what he had to do. To lose him would be disaster—he would be lost in this dead, ugly world. Then he would be dead himself. His feet seemed to adhere to the gritty pavement, and a stiff wind held him back like a hand. As the man receded another several yards down the street, it came to Bunting that what he was following was an angel, not a man, and he cried out in terror. Instantly the being stopped moving and stood with his back to Bunting. The pale robe fluttered about him. A certain word had to be spoken, or the angel would begin walking again and leave Bunting in this terrible world. The word was essential, and Bunting did not know it, but he opened his mouth and shouted the first word that came to him. The instant it was spoken, Bunting knew that it was the correct word. He forgot it as soon as it left his throat. The angel slowly began to turn around. Bunting inhaled sharply. The front of the robe was red with blood, and when the angel held out the palms of his hands, they were bloody, too. The angel's face was tired and dazed, and his eyes looked blind.

XIV

ON TUESDAY MORNING, BUNTING awoke with tears in his eyes for the wounded angel, the angel beyond help, and realized with a shock of alarm that he was in someone else's house. For a moment he was completely adrift in time and space, and thought he might actually be a prisoner in an attic—his room held no furniture except a table and chair, and the windows seemed barred. It came to him that he might have died. The afterlife contained a strong, pervasive odor of soap and disinfectant. Then the bars on the windows resolved into streaks and shadows, and he looked up to the bottles sticking straight out on the wall above his head, and remembered what he had done. The wounded angel slipped backward into the realm of forgotten things where so much of Bunting's life lay hidden, and Bunting moved his legs across the bumpy landscape of baby bottles, his fakir's bed of nails, and pulled himself out of the bed. His legs, shoulders, back, and arms all ached.

Out on the street, Bunting realized that he was enjoying his unemployment. For days he had carried with him always a slight burn of hunger, and hunger was such a sharp sensation that there was a small quantity of pleasure in it. Sadness was the same, Bunting realized—if you could stand beside your own sadness, you could appreciate it. Maybe it was the same with the big emotions, love and terror and grief. Terror and grief would be the hardest, he thought, and for a moment uneasily remembered Jesus slapping a bloody palm against the side of his old house in Battle Creek. Holy holy holy.

The extremely uncomfortable thought came to him that maybe terror and grief were holy, too, and that Jesus had appeared before him in a Battle Creek located somewhere north of Greenwich Village to convey this.

A white cloud of steam vaguely the size and shape of an adult woman rose up from a manhole in the middle of Broadway and by degrees vanished into transparency.

Bunting felt the world begin to shred around him and hurried into Fairway Fruits and Vegetables. He bought apples, bread, carrots, tangerines, and milk. At the checkout counter he imagined the little engine on the cover of the Tolstoy novel issuing white flags of steam and launching itself into the snowstorm. He had the strange sense, which he knew to be untrue, that someone was *watching* him, and this sense followed him back out onto the wide crowded street.

A woman-sized flag of white steam did not linger over Broadway, there was no sudden outcry, no chalked outline to show where a human being had died.

Bunting began walking up the street toward his building. Brittle pale light bounced from the roofs of cars, from thick gold necklaces, from sparkling shop windows displaying compact discs. In all this brightness and activity lurked the mysterious sense that someone was still watching him—as if the entire street held its breath as it attended Bunting's progress up the block. He carried his bag of groceries through the cold bright air. Far down the block, someone called out in a belling tenor voice like a hunting horn, and the world's hovering attention warmed this beautiful sound so that it lingered in Bunting's ears. A taxi slid forward out of shadow into a shower of light and revealed, in a sudden blaze of color, a pure and molten yellow. The white of a Chinese woman's eyes flashed toward Bunting, and her black hair swung lustrously about her head. A plume of white breath came from his mouth. It was as if someone had spoken secret words, instantly forgotten, and the words spoken had transformed him. The cold sidewalk beneath his feet seemed taut as a lion's hide, resonant as a drum.

Even the lobby of his building was charged with an anticipatory meaning.

He let himself into his bare room and carried the groceries to his bed and carefully took from the bag each apple and tangerine, the carrots, the milk. He balled up the bag, took it and the carton of milk to the kitchen alcove, flattened out the bag and folded it neatly, and then poured the milk into three separate bottles. These he took back across his sparkling floor and set them beside the bed. Bunting took off his shoes, the suit he was wearing, his shirt and tie, and hung everything neatly in his closet. He returned to the bed in his underwear and socks. He turned back the bed and got in on top of his fakir's blanket of baby bottles and pulled the sheets and blanket up over his body without shaking off any of the objects on the bed. He doubled his pillow and switched on his lamp, though the cold light from outside still cast large bright rectangles on the floor. He leaned back under the reading light and arranged the fruit, carrots, bread, and bottles around him. He raised one of the bottles to his mouth and clamped the nipple between his teeth. There was a brisk pleasant coolness in the air that seemed to come from the world contained in the illustration on the cover of the book beside him.

Bunting drew in a mouthful of milk and picked up the copy of *Anna Karenina* from the bedside chair. He was trembling. He opened the book to the first page, and when he looked down at the lines of print, they rose to meet his eye.

XV

THE SUPER OF THE BUILDING LOOKED
down as he fit the key into the lock. He turned it,
and both men heard the lock click open. The super
kept looking at the floor. He was as heavy as Bunting's father, and the two sweaters he wore against
the cold made him look pregnant. Bunting's father
was wearing an overcoat, and his shoulders were
hunched and his hands were thrust into its pockets.
The breath of both men came out in clouds white as
milk. Finally the super glanced up at Mr. Bunting.

"Go on, open it up," said Mr. Bunting.

"Okay, but there are some things you probably
don't know," the super said.

"There's a lot I don't know," said Mr. Bunting.
"Like what the hell happened, basically. And I guess
you can't be too helpful on that little issue, or am I
wrong?"

"Well, there's other things, too," the super said,
and opened the door at last. He stepped backward to
let Mr. Bunting go into the room.

Bunting's father went about a yard and a half
into the room, then stopped moving. The super
stepped in behind him and closed the door.

"I fucking hate New York," said Mr. Bunting. "I
hate the crap that goes on down here. Excuse me for
getting personal, but you can't even keep the heat on
in this dump." He was looking at the wall above the
bed, where many of the bottles had been splashed,

instead of directly at the bed itself. The bed had been cracked along a diagonal line, and the sheets, which were brown with dried blood, had hardened so that they would form a giant stiff 'V' if you tried to take them off. Someone, probably the super's wife, had tried to mop up the blood alongside the cracked, folded bed. Chips of wood and bent, flattened bedsprings lay on the smeary floor.

"The tenants are all mad, but it's a good thing we got no heat," the super said. "I mean, we'll *get* it, when we get the new boiler, but he was here ten days before I found him. And I'll tell you something." He came cautiously toward Mr. Bunting, who took his eyes off the wall to scowl at him. "He made it easy for me. See that police bolt?"

The super gestured toward the long iron rod leaning against the wall beside the door frame. "He left it that way—unlocked. It was like he was doing me a favor. If he'd a pushed that sucker across the door, I'd a had to break down the door to get in. And I probably wouldn't have found him for two more weeks. At least."

"So maybe he made it easy for whoever did it," said Bunting's father. "Some favor."

"You saw him?"

Mr. Bunting turned back to look at the bottles above the bed. He turned slowly to look at the bottles on the front wall. "Sure I saw him. I saw his face. You want details? You can go fuck yourself, you want details. All they let me see was his face."

"It didn't look like anybody could have done that," the super said.

"That's real clever. Nobody did it." He saw something on the bed, and moved closer to it. "What's that?" He was looking at a shrivelled red ball that had fallen into the bottom of the fold. A smaller, equally shrivelled black ball had fallen a few feet from it. "I think it's an apple," said the super. "He had some apples and tangerines, some bread. And if you look close, you can see little bits of paper stuck all over the place, like some book exploded. All the fruit dried out, but the book…I don't know what happened to the book. Maybe he tore it up."

"Could you maybe keep your trap shut?" Mr. Bunting took in the bottles above the bed for an entire minute. Then he turned and stared at the unstained bottles on the far wall. At last he said, "This is what I don't get. I don't get this with the baby bottles."

He glanced at the super, who quickly shook his head to indicate that he did not get it either.

"I mean, you ever get any other tenants down here who did this kind of thing?"

"I never seen anyone do this before," said the super. "This is a new one. These bottles, I gotta take the walls down to get' em off."

Mr. Bunting seemed not to have heard him. "First my wife dies—three weeks ago Tuesday. Then I hear about Bobby, who was always a fuck-up, but who happens to be my only kid. When they decide to give it to you, they really give it to you good. They know how to do it. Now on top of everything else, here's this crap. Maybe I should have stayed away."

"You saw his face?" the super asked.

"Huh?"

"You said you saw his face."

Mr. Bunting gave the super the glance that one heavyweight gives another when they touch gloves.

"Well, I did, too, when I found him," the super said. "I think you ought to know this. It's something, anyhow."

Mr. Bunting nodded, but did not alter his expression.

"When I came in…I mean, your son was dead, there was no doubt about that. I was in Korea, and I know what dead people look like. It looked like he got hit by a truck. It's crazy, but that's what I thought when I saw him. He was smashed up against the wall, and the bed was all smashed…Anyhow, what got me was the expression on his face. Whatever happened happened all right, and pardon me, but there's no way the police are ever gonna arrest a couple of guys and get 'em on this, because no couple of guys could ever do what I saw in this room with my own eyes, believe me—"

He inhaled. Bunting's father was looking at him with flat impatient indifferent anger.

"But anyhow, the point is, the way your son looked. He looked happy. He looked like he saw the greatest goddamn thing in the world before *whatever* the hell it was happened to him."

"Oh, yeah," Mr. Bunting said. He was shaking his head. "Well, he didn't look that way when I saw him, but I'm not too surprised by what you say." He smiled for the first time since entering his son's room, and started shaking his head again. The smile made the other man's stomach feel small and cold. "His mother never understood it, but I sure did."

"What?" asked the super.

"He always thought he was some kind of big deal." Mr. Bunting included the whole apartment in the gesture of his arm. "I couldn't see it."

"It's like that sometimes," the super said.